Family Tree (by Bea aged 9 1/2)

Dedication:

For Anthony (1933 – 2008).

For our dearest Rose, Tom and Joe.

For my terrific and funny grandchildren.

Print production by
Gipping Press Ltd: Unit 2, Lion Barn Estate,
Needham Market, Suffolk, IP6 8NZ
Tel: 01449 721599
www.gippingpress.co.uk

Acknowledgements:

There is so much to be thankful for, but in particular I give deep gratitude to my incredible extended family and mutually supportive dear friends over the past 18 months.

With thanks to Yula and my Pop Chorus friends for keeping us all singing and learning.

With thanks to the Button Moon Swimmers, Gill my swimming buddy and Felixstowe Seascapes for inspired encouragement to keep dipping in all weathers!

To Felixstowe Lawn Tennis Club members for their ongoing friendship and fun.

Thanks once again to Catherine Kendal aka 'Pernickety Kate' - my brilliant editor, and also to the great Gipping Press printers.

Chapter 1

'Oi! Watch out Alex, you nearly elbowed me into the water!' 9-year-old Sophia just managed to catch a hanging branch of a tree with both hands as she scrambled on the bank over the fast-moving stream. She clung on desperately while her feet paddled like mad, trying to get a grip on the wet muddy slope. Unable to stop, Alex had just skidded past her.

The deep stream rushed and gurgled along some way below them on their right.

'Well, do get out of the way!' yelled her big brother Alex as he slithered along, unable to control his caked, sliding wellies. 'Aaaargh!' he cried, as one of his feet took a turn down the slope sideways while the other one stayed where it was. He was doing the splits. Sophia, still hanging on to the branch for dear life, started giggling.

Bea and Harry were running behind convulsed with laughter, observing Alex and Sophia's antics. The added knowledge that the brook was icy cold and fast moving filled them with more nervous chuckles.

Game on! The game was called 'paper chase'. The children were way ahead and were using stale cornflakes and oats as a trail for the others to follow.

Rather a lot of the trail had been eaten by the children on the way, and most had gone by the time they got to the 'cut', as the family called it. This was a narrow gorge with a fast-moving brook at the bottom of it. The gorge ran between two sloping fields – a great place for playing racing sticks, or rubber ducks for that matter. A slippery path ran above it.

The idea was that the four children should get back home before they were caught. They had had a good start, but the 'chasers' were catching up fast. Bella and daddy Tom were in front. After them came Ellie with daddy Joe. They were making a good job of chasing.

The rest of the family grown-ups, Rose and Jon, Clare, Dee Dee and granny Gar Gar, were casually strolling along, way back, chattering to each other, paying little attention to the game.

'Quick! They're catching us up!' shouted Harry.

The four children in their waterproofs slid and slipped along, doing their best not to get their wellies stuck or slip over in the mud.

The children had the advantage of knowing where they were going, but it was only a small advantage. Even though they were fast runners, their legs were shorter than the adults', and they were much more likely to take a tumble into the cold murky water.

It was early afternoon on 29th December 2020. A special day for the family. Joe's 39th birthday. Everyone was excited. Sometimes after Christmas, things can feel a little flat, but having a birthday in the family is an excellent way to break up any post-Christmas squashed out feelings.

But oh dear, there had been SO much rain! Floods all over England, Ireland, Scotland and Wales. Poor people marooned in their houses, or worse, having to move out of them. Even parts of usually dry Suffolk had flooded too. All the rivers were swollen with water. Everywhere looked like a wet flannel needing a good wringing out. But the rain was good for the trees and plants which had endured such a drought only 7 months earlier.

The cold day was grey tinged with the occasional luminous streak of silver. Steely rounded clouds hung heavily in the sky, full of rain. Typical winter sunlight – thin and watery. But family spirits were running high.

Alex and Sophia were still ahead of Bea and Harry. There was usually a bit of competition between the siblings, and today was no exception – they each wanted to be the first home. Both fast runners, sometimes Sophia could outrun Alex these days, even though he was 18 months older. But now their rivalry had led to a sticky situation.

Suddenly there was an almighty crack as the branch that Sophia had been hanging onto broke into two.

'Aaargh!' she screamed as she found herself rolling and sliding down the bank towards the icy brook. 'Help!'

She was gathering momentum as she rolled down the side of the bank, trying to grip onto bits of stumps or even old nettles, but to no avail. Splash! She was in! The others, panting, peered over the top of the bank and tried to see where she had gone. She seemed to have disappeared from view. Maybe it was the slope and the vegetation which was hiding her, but they couldn't see her.

'Soph!' yelled Bea. 'Are you there? Where are you? Are you okay?'

But there was absolutely no reply.

'Help! Sophia clung on desperately.'

11

Chapter 2

Harry, Alex and Bea hollered from the top of the bank. 'Sophia! Where are you? Can you hear us? Answer us! SOPH!' As they got no response, they began to panic.

'Come on! We've got to get down there!' exclaimed Harry.

The three of them slid and scrambled down the muddy slope, trying not to fall but ending up on their waterproof, mud-covered backsides, slipping down rapidly towards the water. They only just managed to stop themselves on the bank edge, before they would have plunged into the freezing brook. Anxiously peering over the edge, up and down stream, they couldn't see anything, or anyone. Nothing.

'Oh no! Where is she? Has she been washed down stream?' shouted Alex. 'Soph! where are you?'

A sudden awareness overcame Bea and she looked upwards at a branch on an overhanging tree. There was a small bird sitting and chattering furiously at them, piercing the winter silence. The little creature was making an almighty racket, and seemed to be trying to talk to them. Tiny little whistles interspersed with harsh *tsak tsak*, like the sound of two stones being struck together, seemed to be aimed straight at them. Bea looked at it curiously.

'What IS that little bird doing?' she asked. 'Shhh, listen! It seems very alarmed about something!'

There was a pause as the three children looked upwards and listened intently to the tiny high-pitched whistling voice.

'Oh crikey!' Alex giggled. 'It sounds exactly like Sophia, when she has a lot to say! But come on, we haven't got time for that! The water's freezing and Sophia is in it somewhere. We need to follow the river… Let's go!'

Now the little bird was flying round and round the three children, swooping, diving, its round black head, stripey pale orange feathered chest and bright eyes flashing past them. The twittering, whistling *tsak tsak wheee tsak* call continued in the same agitated way. It was so loud!

And then the strangest thing happened. The three children could clearly hear the words in a high pitched but bossy little voice: 'Jump! Jump! Jump!'

'Holy Mackerel! I think it **is** Soph!' whispered Harry. 'What the…? How come she's a… bird?! She wants us to jump – is she nuts? What, into there?' he stammered, pointing at the freezing, babbling water.

Bea spoke up. ' 'Harry! Alex! That might well be Sophia, and something or someone has turned her into a bird, of all things. What shall we do?'

A creeping sensation came over Alex and Harry. They could feel it in their bellies, a sort of nervous excitement. Alex felt a lurch. He, of all the children, knew that this could only mean one thing. Something was afoot, and likely as not it was something to do with Magic Joe, Ogo Pogo, Ege Pege or even Magic Merry – the magical friends who had led them all on some amazing adventures in recent years.

Just then the three children heard the voices of grown-ups. Tom and Joe were calling out loudly in their deep voices: 'Ho there! We're coming!' And they were getting nearer.

'Come on! Quick!' shouted Bea decisively. Grabbing Alex and Harry by their hands – the little bird still twittering around their heads – with one brave and incredible motion, she leapt into the deep, freezing water.

Urgh, it was cold! – bitingly cold! Alex tumbled downwards as the air in his lungs became a sharp freezing pain. Rushing, gurgling water roared in his ears. There was immense pressure around Bea's body as the icy temperature penetrated every part of it. Harry was being thrown every which way in the freezing babbling water, and everything was spinning. The water stung and stunned them all, and quite quickly, all three children were totally numb.

But thankfully the freezing hell didn't last long. Next was the most amazing lightness and upward motion. They were zooming out of the water and soaring upwards into the sky above. They looked about them and realised they had wings and feathers, were beaked, and each had a voice like the little Sophia bird that had been chattering to them before. Oh, what it was to be dry, warm, light and free! With delighted shrills they swooped about at all angles. They loved it! Flying with your own wings, to go wherever you want, is just the most magical, freeing experience!

'Can you hear me, Soph?' called Alex in his loudest little bird twittering voice.

'Of course I can! You don't need to shout!' chirruped Sophia irritably. 'We're all the same now! Come on, you lot, come and perch on this branch with me. We need to talk!'

And as if they had done it all their lives, Alex, Harry and Bea swooped towards the branch and landed neatly using their little bird claws to perch tightly to the bark of the branch. The four of them sat tidily in a row, turning their heads this way and that winking at each other with their beady little sideways eyes.

But before they had a chance to say anything, the big booming voices of Tom and Joe came crashing along the path just near the branch they were sitting on. Gosh, the men's voices were loud! The little birds on the branch cowered slightly but they did not move. The two men carried on walking past, calling and shouting for the children. Tom could be heard saying to Joe, 'Where have those children got to? We should probably get a move on, so that we don't lose them altogether.'

'Not much sign of any trail now,' said Joe. 'They must have used it all up. Hope we're on the right path!' The two men strode on hurriedly, calling as they went.

The two youngest cousins, Bella and Ellie, had fallen some way back along the path, behind their fathers, discussing the lack of clues for the paper chase.

'Well, really!' exclaimed Bella indignantly. 'We haven't seen any stale cornflakes for ages. Do you think we're still following them – do you think they even came this way? Pooh! I don't think much of this game. How on earth are we supposed to know where they went if they don't leave any clues? They could be anywhere!'

'I agree, there's absolutely no sign of them!' sighed Ellie who was secretly getting a bit tired. Her little legs were aching, with all the slippery sliding that had been going on. She did not like her waterproofs and found her boots too heavy. 'I don't even know for sure that they came this way. I need a rest! Shall we just stay here for a bit and wait for our mums to catch up?'

'Hmm. Not a bad idea,' replied Bella.

Then Bella glanced up and saw the four birds eyeballing her from the branch.

'That's funny,' she thought, *'I could swear those birds are winking at me.'*

Tom and Joe had paced ahead still calling out for the older children.

The four birds swooped down and circled Bella and Ellie's heads chattering to them insistently and noisily.

Ellie stared at them. She wasn't frightened, and took in the little birds in her very perceptive and clever way. 'They're talking to us, Bella!' she exclaimed. 'Those birds are actually talking to us!' It rather reminded her of last summer when she and Bella had cared for all those birds and other little animals in Blaxhall woods. But that's another story.

And then they heard those fateful words coming from the little birds' beaks. High pitched but clear as day: 'Jump! Jump! **Jump!**' Insistent too… the four birds kept repeating, 'Jump! Jump! **Jump!**'

Bella, looking down at the swirling mass of freezing water, thought it was a terrible idea. But then she realised that if they didn't jump pretty soon, their dads would be back to collect them, and then they'd have to carry on walking in the slippery mud with their heavy wellies all clogging up.

Ellie, at the same time, recognised that those birds were no ordinary birds and adored the magical way they were talking to her. They reminded her of something but she couldn't think what. (She almost, but not quite, realised that it was the other children). But she didn't feel the least bit afraid. She suddenly had more energy than she had had all morning.

So, without any discussion, with determination and a silent nod in agreement, Bella and Ellie grabbed each others' hands, and whispered 'One, two, three, **jump**!'

Slipping and sliding all the way down the slope, they bravely leapt straight into the gorge below.

The freezing water stung and stunned them all.

By Alex (11)

Chapter 3

Well, we know what an unpleasant thing that was for Bella and Ellie. It was just as it had been for the other four cousins. Stinging, bitingly cold and blisteringly painful, it was just about the worst experience of their lives. But without describing it all over again, we also know that it was over quite quickly and soon the two smallest birds were out of it, swooping and whistling, chattering and twittering, all fluffed up, just like the other four. And loving it!

After a while flying about and trying out aerial acrobatics for the first time, the six cousins finally came to perch on the branch of the tree and cocked their heads this way and that, peering at each other with their little bright eyes. It is hard to smile with a beak, but if they could have, they would have been grinning broadly.

'Right then,' tweeted Harry. 'Now what? Any ideas, anyone?'

There was rather a long silence. No one had the foggiest idea what they were doing perched on this branch, or what they were supposed to do next either.

'Sophia, how on earth did you first become a bird?' cheeped Bea.

'Well, you know, I fell in the brook and it just happened, like the rest of you. I didn't know it was going to happen, and believe me, I wasn't exactly invited! I could blame you really, Alex, for pushing past me on the path!'

'I couldn't help it, Soph, I was slithering everywhere and I ended up doing the splits anyway!'

The four others twittered helplessly, remembering how funny the two siblings looked.

'Look here,' chirped Harry. 'We need a plan. Jon, our Mums and Gar Gar are about to catch up and walk past, and I think we need to make ourselves scarce. I'm hoping that they will assume we've all gone a long way ahead.'

'Well,' cheeped Bella cleverly. 'They will think Ellie and I are with Tom and Joe. And hopefully Tom and Joe will think Ellie and I fell back to be with our mums. At least that gives us a little time before everyone realises that we've gone missing.'

'Good thinking, Bella,' chirruped Bea. 'I think there's only one thing we can sensibly do. That is to fly to Alex's room and see if Ogo Pogo and Ege Pege are in their matchbox, and hopefully they'll be able to tell us what on earth is going on. And we don't have much time do we!'

Ogo Pogo (pronounced *Ohgo Pohgo*) and Ege Pege (pronounced *Eegee Peegee*) were two tiny elderly creatures about the size of Harry's little finger. With whirls of rather long white hair, they wore little pixie hats and had tiny upturned noses and bright green eyes the colour of the sea. Wearing small mustard-coloured sleeveless jerkins and dark green leggings, they had small bodies and skinny little arms and legs. On their feet they always wore battered old shoes.

The two tiny identical pixie creatures lived in a matchbox on the windowsill in Alex's bedroom at the family home in Parham. Alex and Sophia's mother, Rose, and her two brothers, Tom and Joe, had grown up with Ogo Pogo and Ege Pege. They were able to do some magic, but not that much these days. When they were young, a long time ago, those two had got into all sorts of trouble and adventures.

Exactly eighteen months ago at midsummer, Ogo Pogo had disappeared out of Alex's bedroom window in his Lego aeroplane. It was a near disaster. The cousins had to undertake a dangerous mission to rescue Ogo Pogo before he perished. It was an adventure involving the two knee-high twin elves Magic Joe and Magic Merry.

Then last summer, there had been a terrifying mission with Ogo Pogo, Ege Pege and Magic Joe into Blaxhall Woods where the six cousins had to rescue Magic Merry, who was in all sorts of dreadful trouble.

But those are two different stories, which you can read about another time.

Now it seemed to the six children that they were about to embark on another adventure.

Alex was thinking hard. Did he leave his window open? Hmm, unlikely in this weather. His dad Jon would have been furious if he had! Could they get in? *'Oh dear,'* he thought. *'How are we supposed to get into the house? We can't exactly turn handles with these wings. And even if we do, will Ogo and Ege actually be **in** their match box?'* He could feel his thoughts churning about in disarray. But without a better idea he went along with the others' plan.

'Right let's do it! And quickly!' chirped Sophia urgently.

'They perched on the branch of a tree and cocked their heads this way and that'

Chapter 4

Without any delay, Sophia, followed by the others, set off speedily through the tree tops, swooping and swerving, enjoying every minute of that marvellous flight. They quickly overtook Joe and Tom who were still calling to them from the river bank.

Sometimes overtaking each other, diving and dipping, they darted round branches and twigs in the trees they were flying through. Plummeting then zooming, it was the most exhilarating and fantastic thing any of them had done in their lives.

They loved the way the ground was someway beneath but easy to get to. Ellie discovered that if she kept her beak open, the odd little insect would fly into it, and was a tasty treat. Even though it was winter, they didn't feel cold, they felt alive and happy. They twittered and tweeted with excitement. On the way to the house, they flew over the pond, and each one of the little birds swooped down and gathered a beak full of water to drink as they went.

Soon they were approaching the front of the house and headed for the eaves over Alex's bedroom window.

They lined up on the window ledge outside Alex's bedroom.

Sure enough, the window was firmly shut. Dropping down, they lined up on the window ledge. Perching, they could clearly see, through the window, the little Bryant and May matchbox sitting there in its usual place. But no sign of any activity whatsoever.

There was a gloomy silence as the little birds thought. How could they get into the house?

Sophia took off and circuited the house. She went past every window and door looking for anything open, even a crack. Nothing.

She landed back on the window ledge with the others and shook her head.

They all sat there thinking hard. Beneath them, Pebbles, the 6-month-old, rapidly growing kitten/cat, strolled past nonchalantly, tail twitching, then stopped, looking upwards at the row of tasty little birds above her. They eyeballed her sternly. Luckily there was no sign of Tinkerbelle, the other house cat.

Seeing Pebbles gave Alex an idea. 'I've got it! I know how we can get into the house and upstairs, provided the kitchen doors are open. We can get in through the cat flap!' he chirruped.

'Oh, what? You've got to be joking!' the others twittered nervously.

'You mean,' put in Sophia, 'you want us to fly down to ground level and push open the cat flap with our beaks? Then, assuming that we haven't already been pounced on by Pebbles, trust that Tinkerbelle isn't lying on her bed in the utility room, ready to grab us as we each get inside?' She looked a very grumpy little bird indeed.

'Well, you come up with a better plan then!' cheeped Alex. 'It's not easy being a bird, is it?!'

'I love being a bird!' chirruped Ellie.

Then there was silence as they all thought again.

by Sophia 9½

Sixstone chats

'Can't we prop the cat flap open with something?' trilled Bella.

'And we need to distract Pebbles somehow,' put in Bea. 'Then one of us can get into the house.'

Then Ellie piped up: 'I should go into the house, because I'm the smallest and I'm very fast.'

'That's really brave, Ellie!' Harry chirped. 'But there's no way you're going alone and as I'm your big brother, I think I should come with you to keep you safe.'

So that's what they did. They all swooped down to the back of the house. Alex and Bea found some sticks and managed to wedge open the cat flap. Sophia and Bella twittered about on the garden side, making lots of noise and distracting Pebbles who was whirling about trying to catch the little birds with her paw, tail twitching.

Ellie and Harry darted through the cat flap. Luckily Tinkerbelle was nowhere to be seen and they swooped through the open kitchen doors and straight up the stairs into Alex's room. There on the window sill was the matchbox.

But alas, the matchbox had been slid open, and nothing and nobody was in there.

'Oh NO!' cheeped Harry! 'What do we do?'

Ellie was hopping round the matchbox peering this way and that into it with her bright little eyes.

'Harry, look,' she chirped. 'There's a note, a tiny note.'

Harry hopped closer. Sure enough, there in the bottom of the box lay a tiny piece of paper about the size of a stamp. He picked it up with his beak and laid it on the window sill to scrutinize.

There in the bottom of the matchbox lay a tiny piece of paper, about the size of a stamp.

Chapter 5

There in minute handwriting were the words: 'Gone to find Magic Joe. Redgrave Woods. Something's gone very wrong, come quick.'

Harry read it out loud to Ellie and the two of them looked at each other. 'Come on!' chirped Harry. 'We must go straight away!'

The two little birds, Harry with the note in his beak, swooped down the stairs and through the kitchen at top speed. They darted out into the utility room, dipped their wings through the cat flap and zoomed out into the garden. They soared into the nearest tree, calling to the others to come and join them.

Harry told the others about the note and showed it to them.

'But do we know how to get to Redgrave Woods?' asked Bea. 'In fact, what ARE they?'

Alex thought for a minute. Hadn't his mum Rose often mentioned playing in the woods at Redgrave when she was a little girl? 'Isn't Redgrave near a town called "This"? You know, where Mummy, Tom and Joe grew up?'

Sophia looked thoughtful. Then her eyes lit up. 'I remember! It's "Diss", not "This"!'

Harry nodded his head in agreement adding that he thought it was in the next county northwards, Norfolk.

'Well! I wonder – just how did Ogo Pogo and Ege Pege get there without their flying matchbox?' chirped Bea.

No one knew how to answer that very sensible question.

'And, oh dear!' cheeped Bella, 'Is it a long way away? What will we find when we get there? How will we let the grown-ups know where we are?'

'Well,' replied Alex, 'you know how time always stands still here while we are off on a magical adventure! But we should leave them a sign, just in case.'

After a good deal more discussion amongst the little birds, Harry agreed to fly upstairs again, fetch the empty matchbox in his beak, and place that, with the note in it, in the middle of kitchen table. That was the best thing they could think of.

The children guessed that at least Rose, Tom and Joe would worry less if they saw the note. They knew about the sort of magic that can happen as a result of Ogo Pogo and Ege Pege being in the house. They'd had fair warning all their lives.

Chapter 6

The six little birds set off.

They'd already done a lot of squabbling as to which way to go. There was a fairly noisy exchange of cheeping, chirping, tweeting and fluttering about. But they were really none the wiser.

All they knew was that it was in the opposite direction from Blaxhall, Aldeburgh, and the River Alde; places they definitely knew how to get to. They had driven to Redgrave with their mums and dads a few times. But of course, hardly any children in their right minds will take the blindest bit of notice of road numbers or directions.

The only thing they knew for certain was that Redgrave was the opposite direction to the sea and that Norfolk was further north.

They decided in the end to fly to Framlingham town and see if they could find a sign post to read. At least they all knew the way there. They thought they should go north west from there (if they could work out which way that was!). Alex was kicking himself that he couldn't carry his little compass. But wings are no good for that kind of thing!

Swooping and dipping, they followed the old railway line that runs from Parham to the town. Sometimes they dipped below the tree line and plummeted towards the ground, snatching tiny flying insects to eat as they flew. Another time they came to a small stream and swooped down for a drink. Up and over the trees again, they very soon found they were in Framlingham. It had taken them no time at all! They were thrilled. Flying was just great!

There was a greyness about the streaky sky and Ellie wondered if it was going to rain again. She began to wonder what happens to birds when it rains. Are they waterproof?

Circling the old castle walls, they tried to find some signposts. They landed on one that was on a fork in the road. The six little cousin birds perched on it and looked down. It's jolly hard for a bird to read, you know. Their eyes are on the sides of their heads and they can't look forwards or focus like we can. Their heads were turning this way and that, trying to decipher the words, which, incidentally, were also upside down to them!

'Oh! for goodness' sake, this is really annoying!' squawked Sophia irritably. And she took off and circled around the sign post fluttering about till she could at last read one of the words.

She landed back on the sign, 'EYE,' she announced.

'EYE? Eye what?' questioned Alex, feeling justifiably confused.

'Just EYE,' she chirped firmly.

At which point all the little birds got the most dreadful giggles. 'I! I!' they all started chirruping. I don't know if you've ever heard birds giggling, but they do sound very funny indeed, with their high pitched little chattering noise. None of them had a clue what Sophia meant when she said 'EYE' as they thought she meant 'I'. There was a great deal of interrupted debating and trilling.

'Oh DO come on!' Eventually Sophia lost patience and swiftly, because her bird senses told her that the road was heading north west, she zoomed off in the direction of the signpost for EYE and the others followed on, still twittering.

It must have been a few miles on that the six little cousin birds began to feel rather tired. Bella and Ellie, the smallest birds were lagging behind somewhat. Alex circled back to them and checked their progress. It seemed they needed a rest.

It had been becoming increasingly gloomy. A chill in the air had begun to be noticeable, even with feathers, and there was now no sunlight. The birds had an almost irresistible feeling that they ought to stop? What was going on?

Finding a large tree on the side of the lane, they flew up into the middle of it and perched on a sturdy branch in a row, eyeballing each other.

Harry chirped up, 'Hey, guys, are you feeling sleepy?'

The others nodded.

'I wonder,' continued Harry. 'You know how birds all settle on branches to roost when it gets dark – well maybe that's what Nature does. It tells them to do that, to rest. And because we're birds now, that's what we're feeling. It's something we can't ignore – a desire to find a safe place to sleep for the night, until dawn comes.'

'Well, anyway, I can hardly see anything now,' agreed Bea. 'I've just been following Alex and Sophia. Pity we're not owls, then we would be able to see at night and catch things to eat too.'

Bella piped up sleepily, 'It is getting dark, and I'm cold – I need to put my head inside my wing like this!' And before anyone knew it, she had her head under her wing and was snoring slightly. Ellie followed suit, snuggling up on her perch next to Bella.

The older four looked at each other and blinked. There was not much they could do –they were quickly being sucked into sleep by the force of Nature. So they did likewise. They pivoted slightly, so that they were sitting diagonally along the branch. They didn't know why they did that, but it felt the right thing to do. Perhaps there would be less chance of them toppling off. They edged nearer each other for warmth. It seemed like it might be a long night.

A few other birds landed on nearby branches, shook themselves, preened a little, and then, putting their heads under their wings too, fell asleep.

Darkness descended, the wind rustled and far away a wise old barn owl hooted.

Chapter 7

In the depth of the night, as the little group slept soundly, the wind got up.

A storm was approaching from the north east. In our Suffolk winters, this is the wind direction everyone loathes. It is a hateful. Aptly called 'The Beast from the East', biting freezing wind come straight from the Arctic and Russia. Moving across Scandinavian countries it is sucked towards east coast Suffolk. Unfortunately, it can last for days or even weeks on end. It makes walking by the sea a really horrid experience. Spurred on by the direction of the wind and currents at high tide, huge waves can lash the beaches depositing a lethal mixture of spray and stones. The sometimes-accompanying rain is stingingly cold.

Now, in the tree, the rustling of the few remaining leaves became more of a shaking. The branches began to sway from side to side. The birds slept on. As the wind began to howl through the branches it got colder. The little birds shifted slightly on their perches, adjusted their clawed grip in their sleep. The wind really started swinging through the tree now, and the branches were whipping around. And then the rain came. Not heavy at first, but blowing steadily through the tree with the wind. At an angle it came. Gradually it got louder. It drummed and thrummed the ground around the tree. It splashed and bounced off the branches and twigs. The noise was fantastic.

'Aargh!' Bea had woken up to find herself being swung from side to side by wind. She was getting a soaking. Clinging on to the branch for dear life, her little voice squawking as loudly as it could, she tried to alert the others.

'Wake up! Wake up!' she crowed, crying to them in her alarm voice, trying to summon them.

The birds all awoke and began twittering at once... little squawking, calling voices, agitated and alarmed; 'Aargh!' 'Help!' 'I'm getting drenched!' 'What shall we do? What shall we do?'

They clung tightly to the branch. Then Harry suddenly couldn't hold on any longer, and blew away with the wind, dropping down to the ground near the main trunk of the tree.

'Harry!' squawked Ellie. And then she too let go and followed Harry down to the base of the tree. The others followed. Soon they were all cowering on the ground out of the wind in the lee of the tree trunk.

'Come on! Get closer!' chirped Harry. And the six little birds nestled up together in a small hollow of the tree. It wasn't really much better, as a pool of water started collecting beneath them. They were all cold and their feathers were getting a good soaking.

Ellie started feeling anxious. She was only little and didn't feel she could cope with the noise, the cold and the rain. She shut her eyes tightly, hoping it would go away. Bella wasn't feeling much better about it either.

Sophia began to feel grumpy. Getting irritable was always Sophia's absolutely best 'go to' place, if she was fearful or upset. She found it usually made her feel stronger and better. She started to think hard, and they were very grumpy thoughts indeed.

Chapter 8

'Blinking storm! That's all we need!' Sophia was thinking. *'Here we are in the middle of nowhere, and it's still practically dark! We have no idea what's going on, or what we're meant to be doing. Supposing that owl sees us and thinks we'd make nice breakfast for him? Honestly! I'll have words with Magic Joe when we see him again – if we do!'*

Perhaps by now you are wondering who Magic Joe was?

Well, Magic Joe was a small, cheerful pixie boy about 20 centimetres tall. He had a big smile and a cheeky expression. Under his mass of sticky out black hair, he had brown sparkling eyes, funny pointy ears and a dirty face. Laurel leaves served as a pair of tatty trousers, and he wore a jacket of woven grass. In a shoulder bag, also made from two leaves stitched together, he carried all kinds of treasures including his very own home-carved magic wand which he used in times of dire need. He wore turned up little shoes which were always rather dirty.

Magic Joe had a twin sister Mary, known as Magic Merry because she was such a jolly and kind little pixie. Exactly the same size as her brother, she had a mop of golden curls and the same funny pointy ears. She wore skirts made from leaves and flowers and usually wore a green mossy cap on her head. You could often see her carrying a small basket of her collections of flowers and herbs. She was much tidier than Magic Joe – everything about her was spick and span. Everybody loved Merry – she was just so sweet and, well, merry! She spent all her time administering help to any sickly animals in the woods. She made her own medicinal cures from the berries, nuts, herbs and flowers that she gathered around her tree house in the forest.

Magic Joe and Magic Merry had already involved the children in some exciting magical adventures, so Sophia was sure they were part of it this time. After all, children don't usually just turn into birds! But how could they find out for sure? Then she had another thought: *'Oh gosh! Yes of course! Magic Joe! That's it! We need to make a spell! We need to use our own little bit of magic to get some help! '*

She jabbed at Alex's neck with her beak, and then shouted in his ear to be heard over the storm.

'Alex! We need to make a spell to get us out of here.'

'Oi! That hurt! What?' chirped Alex.

'MAKE A SPELL!' yelled Sophia in her loudest cheep. Alex nodded.

Sophia jabbed at Bea on the other side of her. 'Bea! We must make a spell to escape from here!'

Bea nodded vigorously, jabbing Harry, and turning to Bella and Ellie, shouted in her noisiest cheep, 'We've got to make a spell!'

'I beg your pardon, Bea?' chirped Harry over the howling of the wind. 'What sort of smell?'

'NO! Not a smell, you idiot! A SPELL!' Now Bea wasn't sure whether to laugh or cry.

'Oh! Okay!' twittered the others.

Alex, who was good at rhyming poems, started in his loudest chirping voice:

'Magic Joe, come help us please…. er… A storm is raging in these trees. There's real danger all about… um…' He paused, stumped for words.

So Harry added:

'We need your help to get us out.'

Bea nudged him. 'That should do it!' she chirped through the wind and rain. 'Now come on everyone, let's say it together in our loudest bird voices and don't forget the ending we always do…'

And so they did. At the top of their voices, they all recited:

'MAGIC JOE, COME HELP US PLEASE,

A STORM IS RAGING IN THESE TREES.

THERE'S REAL DANGER ALL ABOUT,

WE NEED YOUR HELP TO GET US OUT.

NOW'S THE TIME, RENEWED BY SUN,

TO COUNT OUR BLESSINGS ONE BY ONE.'

Bella was just gloomily wondering exactly what 'blessings' they were supposed to be counting right now, when there was a sudden crashing sound through the leaves and branches, as something large and white swooped down, landing clumsily right there, only a metre from them.

Everyone screamed.

The rain splashed and bounced off the branches and twigs.

Chapter 9

'Holy Horses!' squawked Harry. 'It's Ray!'

The huge white bird strutted round the forlorn little group, eyeing them up.

Ray, large and strong, was bright white, except for grey wings. He was quite stout, with a longish yellow bill, yellow legs and webbed feet. He was one of Magic Joe's best animal friends. Magic Joe loved Ray the Seagull, and the seagull loved Magic Joe. They helped each other out of many a scrape. Magic Joe often rode on Ray's back as they flew from place to place.

The little cousin birds hopped round Ray the seagull, overjoyed to see him. Gosh! He looked enormous to them now. Ray peered at each of them with his beady eyes. He took in their bedraggled and forlorn appearance. How tired, battered and hungry they looked! The howling wind and rain were still raging on. Even Ray was feeling a little damp in places. He stood on the leeward side of the base of the chestnut tree, out of the wind, opened his wings and beckoned all the little birds to come to him. They quickly hopped into the awning of Ray's huge whiteness. He closed his warm feather wings around them and they immediately found themselves cocooned in a slightly fishy smelling, feathery duvet of quiet, warmth and darkness. It was delicious. They put their heads under their own wings and immediately drifted into an early morning snooze. Ray squatted on the ground with his 'chicks' under him, and shut his eyes.

The little birds dreamed of warm beds and soft pillows. Comforting sunshine and warmth, their favourite food and fabulous family parties, balloons and birthday cake.

An hour or two later, the little birds gradually woke up. They had a feeling it was time! None of them understood why this happened, but they just felt it. Finding themselves still cocooned in a warm dark place, they stretched and pushed their little bird heads out to see if they could see what was going on. Some birds in the tree above them were singing. Bella recognised one of them. It was a robin with a red breast, making a lovely rich warbling sound.

A streak of silver light could be seen on the horizon, a luminous line cutting across the grey clouds. Dawn. Thankfully, the wind had dropped somewhat and the rain had ceased, but it was still jolly cold.

Dear Ray was still snoozing, towering above them. Feeling the movement under him, he blinked one eye open and peered at the little group who were pushing their way out from beneath him. Waddling clear of them on his webbed feet, he stretched his wings, flapped them and yawned. He wagged his tail feathers.

Opening his beak, he made a huge seagull cry that thoroughly woke up all the small birds.

Sophia and Alex twittered around him while Harry and Bea took off and flew around the tree, landed on a nearby branch and began tweeting together making a dawn chorus. Bella and Ellie stretched their wings and chirruped as they pecked at the ground looking for insects to munch. It was a beautiful moment. The little cousin birds were grateful to be alive!

Sophia landed near to Ray and began quizzing him in her twittering little bird song. 'Ray! It's great to see you! Thank you SO much for rescuing us, we are SO relieved! Amazing that our spell worked! But **please** can you tell us what's going on. Why are we birds? What sort of birds, even? And why are we trying to get to Redgrave, which is in the middle of nowhere? How are Magic Joe and Magic Merry, are they alright? And where on earth are Ogo Pogo and Ege Pege? We are worried about them! Especially as they haven't got their match box with them!'

Those were a lot of questions for a bird like Ray, who wasn't particularly good at quick thinking. He cleared his throat, nodding to the little birds to all come nearer.

'Well,' he squawked in his grating voice with its Suffolk seaside accent, 'first things first. You have been changed into birds by Magic Joe. You are stonechats, which are chatty little birds who are adventurous, brave and clever. You may have heard their bird song before... sometimes the sound is like two stones being struck together! You are birds because you need to be in disguise, and be able to see what is going on without being noticed. Once more, children, Magic Joe needs your help.'

'*Oh dear,*' thought Bella. '*I do hope this won't last too long – the school holidays are over next week and I like going to school!*'

Ray continued, 'Do you remember last summer when you helped capture the goblin that was creating so much evil in Blaxhall woods? Well, Magic Joe and Magic Merry have been working really hard to help him become better-natured and less wicked. They have shared wholesome natural foods with him and given him plenty of useful things to do around the woods, and he did what they asked. They spent a good deal of time in the past months including him in conversations, trying to get him to talk about his past, his life and his parents. But things have not being going very well. He simply clammed up, kept going quiet on them and would not tell them anything. He's not the chattiest creature at the best of times. But lately he became sullen and silent, grumpy and bad tempered every time Magic Joe and Magic Merry tried to talk to him.'

Ray paused, stretched his neck and ruffled his feathers, as if gathering his thoughts for the next stage of the story. This was a long speech for him.

'Now he has run away to Redgrave Woods which is where he grew up as a small goblin. Magic Joe and I followed him there and have observed that he seems to be trying to find something or someone. But if he sees us, he won't talk to us or let us help. He just runs away. Magic Joe doesn't simply want to put a spell on him. He wants to try and get to the bottom of the problem. But the goblin refuses to let Magic Joe near him, or Magic Merry for that matter. They think that the goblin is on a quest of some sort, always looking for something. And we have discovered that he lived in Redgrave woods at exactly the same time as Rose, Tom and Joe when they were children.'

'What! What do you mean, Ray?' chirped Bea, looking alarmed.

'Well,' continued Ray. 'Rose, Tom and Joe were living in the village of Redgrave when they grew up. They lived in Half Moon Lane. At the end of Half Moon Lane were some woods, and the children – that's your mummy Rose, your daddies Tom and Joe, all played in those woods, nearly every day they could. The goblin and his family lived in a tree root near an old ice house.

'An ice house? What on earth was that?' chirped Alex.

'It was a cave deep into the ground that food and ice were lowered into, to keep cool. The people at the country house used to have big parties and they kept everything cold down there so that it wouldn't go off. No one had fridges in those days. It was a brick tunnel, like a well really. Rather deep. Your parents loved playing around there.'

'But that could have been dangerous for them!' chirped up Alex. 'Surely they didn't play in the woods on their own?'

'Yes, they did!' replied Ray. 'Most children had much more freedom in those days. I think they had wonderful adventures and mostly nothing went wrong. But we have a feeling that we have to go back there to discover what did happen to the goblin at that time. That's why you have to be birds; so that you can go back in time and not be children and not be seen.'

'Crikey! Do you mean to say,' whistled Harry, 'that we are going to see our dads and mums when they were children?'

'Well, we might,' squawked Ray. 'It depends. But we need to make sure that they don't see you! You won't have been born yet!'

'Golly' cheeped Ellie. 'This is quite confusing!'

'Well, never mind Ellie!' replied Sophia. 'Let's just get on with it and go!'

'But Ray!' chirped Bella. 'Are we all flying there? We'll never keep up with you, and we don't know the way!'

Those were a lot of questions for a bird like Ray.

Chapter 10

Ray winked at them and perched down onto the ground. 'Come on! Up you all get!' he squawked. Without a second's hesitation, the birds all hopped onto his back and took positions clear of his wings so that he could fly. They clasped onto a few feathers each with their sharp little claws. Without any further ado Ray stood up, spread his wings wide, flapped and took off almost vertically. The cousins were enthralled. They felt perfectly safe. After all, if they slipped off, they could just flap their own wings, fly for a bit, re-land on his back, and would never fall to the ground.

The little birds all hopped onto Ray's back.

It was cold, but exhilarating to be flying so fast on the back of Ray. He had a lovely movement, first beating his wings, and then gliding along, his feet tucked under his body. He purposefully kept his flight level and smooth, his beady eyes always looking around him, up and down, checking for predators or dangers. The small birds on his back surveyed the land below them. There were small clusters of houses, gathered in villages, often a church spire, village greens, small worm-like grey roads, cars that looked like dinky toys going along on them. Miniature people out walking dogs that looked like ants. A bird's eye view really is most interesting!

After a while, the cousins saw a large house and some outbuildings below them, with a bunch of chickens running around and some cows. Ray started a descent.

The little birds wondered what was going on as Ray landed in the farmyard. 'Breakfast time I think!' he winked at them.

There, on a bird table in the garden of the farmhouse, were some wonderful things to eat – some breadcrumbs, some grain, a few raisins and sultanas, dried apple rings, small pieces of cheese. There was a hanging net with some peanuts in it, and another bird feeder full of sunflower seeds. Apart from the balls of fat that hung from a hook on the table, everything there was the kind of thing the cousins enjoyed eating even when they **weren't** birds. But as birds, they liked the fat-balls too. They fell on the food, fluttering and trilling about the bird table, hoovering the delicious morsels up as if they were starving (which they were). A bowl of water sat on a plinth and the birds all clustered around it to get a drink and splash about to clean their feathers. It seemed most natural to them, and it was a whole lot of fun splashing each other, even though the water was so cold!

The farmer and his wife, Jim and Fran, were at the kitchen table having scalding hot coffee, toast and thick-cut chewy marmalade. They loved their home-made brown bread and marmalade in the mornings – their own recipe of Seville marmalade, famous at the village fete. A lovely large window gave them a view into their garden.

'Golly gosh!' exclaimed Fran. 'Look at those birds Jim, there are so many of them feeding off our bird table. I say, what an extraordinary sight!'

Jim got up and went to the front porch, grabbing his binoculars off the hooks by the door.

'Well, I'll be…!' replied Jim the farmer in his Suffolk lilt. 'They're feeding on it like a load of locusts! Whatever's going on? Tell you what, Fran, they're not normal birds – tits and wot not – they look like littly marsh birds to me. Just a minute…'

Fran joined Jim in the doorway as he adjusted the focus on his binoculars to get a better look.

'Say, Fran! They're stonechats, that's what they are! Whatever are they a-doin' around here so far inland?'

Stealthily, the two of them crept a little nearer within ear shot. What they heard made them doubt their sanity.

Tiny little bird voices could clearly be heard speaking tiny cheeping human words. 'Ooh! I say, Alex, this is yummy grub isn't it? Wow! Apple rings! Delish, my favourite! Harry look, there's some cheese! Oi, move over Bella, you've got to share! Mmmm, raisins! Look Ellie! breadcrumbs! **Oooh!** Fat-balls, yum yum! Look Sophia! **Oooh**, Bea – fat-balls are delicious, try some!'

The farmer and his wife stared and listened without believing what they were hearing. Jim pinched his arm to see if he was dreaming. Fran nudged his arm and pointed towards the hen-run. They could see a large white bird strutting around in it, looking as if he owned the place.

'Blinking seagull!' exclaimed Fran. 'Look! It's eating all our chicken food – and I've only just fed the hens!'

Ray had located the chicken pellets to munch, and found some bread crusts that the farmer's wife had just thrown in. The chickens looked grumpily at him.

'Sorry, sisters,' said Ray in chicken language, 'I am most obliged to you for sharing your food.' He winked at the chickens, trying to look charming. They were not impressed.

Then Ray took some long drinks from the hopper full of water. He watched the small bird cousins and smiled to himself.

A fat tabby cat came lazily round the corner, its tail twitching. Ray spotted it immediately and flew over to the bird table. 'Come on! Time to go!' he squawked.

Then, to the amazement of the dazed farmer and his wife, all the little birds swiftly flew up in a small flock and landed neatly on the seagull's back. Then, with all the birds riding on his back, it soared away across the garden, in a north-westerly direction.

'Well! Would you believe it, Fran! I never seen anything like that in my whole life, and I was born 'ere!' exclaimed Jim.

'Definitely something magical going on this morning!' replied Fran, wringing her hands. 'And I'm not sure if I like it. Come on, back inside, Jim. Our coffee's getting cold and it's freezing out here.'

The birds were really hungry!

Chapter 11

In relative comfort with warm, full bellies, the birds rode on Ray's back for quite a while. It was a pleasant journey of about 20 miles. The wind seemed to be mostly coming from behind and to the right of them, as they headed north-westerly inland. Not needing to follow roads via Eye or Diss, Ray flew in a straight line – 'as the crow flies', as the saying goes. Though this time, it was 'as the seagull flies'! Within the hour they had arrived in the village of Redgrave.

A quiet little picturesque backwater of a village, Redgrave had a wonderful historic church, a Methodist church, a community church, a pub, a shop, and a Victorian village school. On the outskirts of the village was the source of the river Waveney and the Little Ouse. This was at Redgrave and Lopham Fen. When they were children Rose, Tom and Joe (now the mum and dads of the six cousins) remembered that a very famous spider called the 'Raft' spider was first discovered there. There was a lovely village green with a pond. The Cross Keys pub next to the village green was a great place to go and sit and feed the ducks with bread crusts, of a summer's evening.

A few miles from Diss, Redgrave was where the siblings Rose, Tom and Joe, spent quite a bit of their childhoods.

They lived in a thatched cottage aptly called Rose Cottage, in a lane called Half Moon Lane. Half Moon Lane ran out of road a few cottages further on from Rose Cottage, just past Dennis Farm house. The lane turned into a track which the family could walk down to get to the famous St Mary's parish church. On the left of the track were acres of wild open fields. On the right of the track were the woods called Tangle Woods.

When Rose, Tom and Joe were growing up, there was more freedom than children seem to have nowadays. The three children would play out in the lane, or in the fields, or go off down to the village shop by themselves, and their parents wouldn't worry about them. For one thing, because Half Moon Lane was a dead end, there were few cars likely to go down as far as Rose Cottage. Secondly, everybody knew everyone else. People looked out for children, knew their names. And thirdly, there were no internet stories about the dreadful things that happen in the world.

So Rose, Tom and Joe got up to all sorts of games and pranks. They would set up shop on the lane, often cheekily selling off each other's toys and books to passing walkers. Home-grown apples and plums would be sold, along with penny buns they baked. They would play tennis and football in the lane and ride their bikes or scooters, play on their roller skates and generally have a wonderful time. There was a rather wild back garden too, adding an extra dimension to their already fabulous playing life.

The woods, however, did hold some anxiety for their parents. They were called Tangle Woods with reason – so very thickly planted with trees that it was easy to get lost and difficult to find your way in and out of. And then, of course, there was the ice house in the middle. That was what caused the children's parents the most worry.

The ice house was an old red-brick vaulted man-made cave – rather like a small air-raid shelter but with a domed ceiling, built over 200 years ago. It had been constructed in the grounds of the big house, called Redgrave Park. The ice house was built in the woods for storing ice blocks to keep fresh meat cool. Although the entrance to the ice house was above ground, it had a tunnel at the front that led down to a deep and dark cellar. There was a make shift door at the start of the ice house, but after that it was a vertical drop, rather like a well, into cold blackness. It was a long way down. Ice and food were lowered using a pulley system. The ice house was mounded in earth so that it was hard to find. Poking out of the top was a chimney which was used, not for fires, but to give air to the cellar.

Rose, Tom and Joe's parents would often discuss whether to ban the children from playing in Tangle Woods. Both parents, Deb and Anthony, had some misgivings about them playing there alone – after all, they could get lost or tangled up or worse still, fall down the ice hole. But in the end, the parents came to the conclusion that the more they banned the children from the woods, the more likely it would be that they would desperately want to play there. Besides, if the children stayed together, they would surely be alright?

When questioned about the woods, the children would always reply, 'Don't worry! We know our way about! And we stick together!' And that was true. But of course, because it was so dangerous, it was THE absolute favourite place the three children loved to play.

The Ice House in Tangle woods.

Chapter 12

The six little cousin birds decided to fly the last bit themselves. Following Ray, they stretched their little wings and fluttered along Half Moon Lane.

The cottages (many of which were thatched) were very pretty, each one different. People were taking great pride in their homes and the little birds could imagine just how charming the lane would be in the spring and summer. Presently they came to a white thatched cottage with a green gate and green painted windows. It had the name 'Rose Cottage' painted on the gate. They all perched on the fence looking into the front garden at the green stable front door.

'Well!' cheeped Alex, eyeballing Sophia.' This is where our Mum grew up! Lovely, isn't it!' Sophia nodded vigorously.

'Ooh yes!' chirped Bea. 'Really pretty! I bet our daddy Tom loved it here!'

'Dad often talks about it!' twittered Harry, and the others all started telling each other little snippets of information about their parents.

And then just as the birds were chattering, the top of the green stable front door creaked open and a blond, bobble-hatted head poked over the top of it. Then the bottom of the door opened too, and a small but sturdy-looking boy in wellies, waterproof trousers, a duffle coat and a woolly hat emerged outside. He had such a healthy glow about him, strong and happy.

'Come on, Rose! Hurry up,' the little boy shouted. 'Get a move on or it might start raining again! Don't forget to bring the stuff.'

'I'm coming, Tom!' and then as an addition the voice from inside the front door called out 'Joe! Where are you? We're ready to go!'

'Wait for me!' shouted a third voice from further inside.

And then before the little birds knew what was happening, two more children, a blonde girl, and a smaller blond boy came running outside also well dressed up for the winter weather. Three blond-haired children, all with blue eyes and all quite close in size. They stood in a row putting on their hats and gloves. A girl of about 10 years old, the first boy they had seen, about 9 years old and a smaller boy about 7 or 8. There was no mistaking that they were a sister and two brothers. They all looked so alike, bursting with health and rosy-cheeked. The girl was carrying a small, red lunchbox. It wasn't made of plastic; it was more like leather or cardboard.

The children stopped and glanced at the birds on the fence for several seconds. Something seemed to register with the children for a few moments. They didn't know why they were staring. Just for a little while, their eyes seemed to connect with the little birds' beady eyes, but it was a fleeting time that didn't last.

'Look at those birds!' exclaimed the girl, whose name was Rose. 'What are they doing sitting in a row on our fence there? Are they robins? Isn't that odd? Look, they're all lined up!'

No-one said anything for a few moments. 'Oh, never mind!' replied the older boy, called Tom. 'Come on let's go to the woods!'

'Yes! Come on!' shouted Joe, the younger boy. 'Race you!'

The next thing the birds knew, the three children were running away down the lane towards Tangle Woods, splashing through the muddy puddles, laughing, calling, and running as fast as they could.

The children stopped and glanced at the birds for a few moments.

Chapter 13

'Holy mackerel!' whistled Harry. 'Were those children who I think they were?'

'Yes!' answered Sophia, 'Harry, that was my mum! And Tom, and your dad Joe!'

'Oh! I can't believe it!' cheeped Bella to Bea. 'That's our daddy Tom as a little boy. He looks about your age, Bea. Oh! He looks such fun. I wish we could play with him!'

'I know Bella! Isn't it just the weirdest thing?' chirped Bea.

Harry had been pondering. 'We must have travelled back in time, more than 30 years! How and when did that happen? Our dad had such blond hair... a bit like mine!'

'I know, Harry, I think you look a lot like our daddy,' twittered Ellie.

Alex was feeling emotional. He didn't know why. It was seeing his special Mummy as a girl, about the age he was then. It was such a strange thing and she looked so sweet, and had such kind eyes. He looked at Sophia and could see that her eyes were watering too.

Sophia swallowed hard as she saw the children diverting off the track to the right. 'Quick, look! They're heading into the woods. Ray, what shall we do?'

'Follow the children, and see what happens!' squawked Ray. 'Stay as close as you can, but **don't** let them know you're there, whatever you do. They mustn't know you're following them. I'm going to see if I can find Magic Joe to tell him we've arrived!'

And with that Ray took off and flew away across above the tree tops. He was soon a white dot moving off into the grey sky.

The three children, Rose, Tom and Joe, moved nimbly through the trees, dodging and diving deeper and deeper into Tangle Woods. They didn't hesitate, it was obvious they knew the way very well. They were followed by the six small birds, silently winging their way after them, making sure they were not struck by any branches or twigs.

Before too long, the children arrived at the ice house. It was indeed rather like a cave but with a hole that headed down hill very steeply – more like a well, in that respect.

The children pulled back the makeshift door and peered down it.

'Hello! Are you there?' Tom's voice echoed as he called down the hole. He had a small torch which he shone down it. 'I can't see anything,' he muttered.

'Hi! It's us!' called young Joe.

'We've brought you something delicious to eat!' shouted Rose more loudly. 'We've brought you some of Joe's birthday cake! We want to help you!'

The six birds perched on the tree nearby, couldn't believe their ears. 'Oh no, this feels bad,'' whispered Bea to the others.

The three children pulled on the rusty chain pulley system, hand over hand, and a plank of wood appeared from inside the tunnel. Attached to the chain at the corners on both ends, the plank was rather like a tray or a swing seat. It was obviously what had been used to lower foods to the cold inside of the ice house in the old days.

The birds' feathers ruffled up in terror when they saw Joe, the smallest boy, sit on the seat with the food in the small red lunchbox and ask Rose and Tom to lower him in. He didn't look a bit scared. It was as if he had done it before. Which he had, naughty boy.

'Don't let me go, will you!' he exclaimed. 'And pull me back up when you feel a tug or hear me shout!'

'Tom and I have got you, don't worry,' said Rose. 'But be careful, Joe. Don't let go of the chains and when you get there, don't get too close… We just can't trust him. Pitch the food at him. Don't let him have my lunchbox, I need it for school. Find out what we can do to help him.'

Tom handed Joe the torch which he put in his pocket, while clutching the food box. This he put between his legs, then he hung on tightly to the chains, and was lowered down into the tunnel. Tom was puffing hard. He seemed to be taking most of the weight while Rose helped but was otherwise busy calling to Joe. 'Are you okay, Joe? Can you see anything?'

It was dark down there. The walls were made of bricks and as the pulley went down it got colder. Joe didn't particularly like going down there, but he knew it had to be him because Tom and Rose were the ones with the strength to pull him up quickly, if necessary. The three children had been down the tunnel once or twice, but they only ever did as a dare, and none of them really liked it. Joe could hear Rose's voice, but as he descended, it grew quieter and quieter, and echoed. Joe fished the small torch out of his pocket and shone it around and downwards. The brick walls were green with mildew and moss. They dripped a little. It really wasn't a nice place to be. He shone the torch to the bottom of the tunnel, peering hard to find what he was looking for. He shivered.

Yesterday afternoon, Rose Tom and Joe had been playing forty-forty in the woods. They had been having a marvellous time. It was a great game – Rose was 'it' and Tom and Joe had been trying to get back to the ice house which was 'home'. Tom had gone round the back of it hoping to creep over the top while Rose was looking for Joe. Picking his way through the undergrowth, Tom had become aware of a dreadful smell; a revolting mixture of sick and dog poo, and then a gobbling, crunching sound. He had caught a glimpse of something moving. And there, with its back to Tom, busily eating a dead mouse, was a goblin.

It was a young goblin – probably in human terms about the same age as Tom, though much smaller. He was absolutely hideous, with greenish slimy skin, red eyes, a beaked nose, sharp pointed teeth, claws on his hands and feet. And that appalling smell seemed to be all around him.

Ages ago, Tom had heard rumours about a family of goblins who were supposedly living in the woods – a fearsome group, always ravenous, with an appetite for the flesh of any living creature. They were said to boil up children and devour them if they got the chance. But despite the gruesome tales, the three children had never seen any goblins, and gradually over time had forgotten all about them.

But now there was no doubt that the stories were true. Tom was horrified and had to take a deep breath to stop himself from screaming. But he was a very brave boy. He didn't scream, but dashed and hid behind the nearest tree intending to follow the goblin. It had finished crunching the mouse, and started mounting the back of the mound covering the ice house, exactly where Tom had been planning to go. He realised that if the goblin actually got to the top, he would be able to see over it, to Rose and Joe. Then they would be in great danger. So, Tom did the only thing he could think of.

Grabbing a large long stick, he charged up the mound following the goblin, yelling at the top of his voice as if he was a warrior. It was like the battle cry of an angry elephant! Making as much noise as he could, he swung the stick round his head as he went. The young goblin was so surprised that he stumbled and slipped, rolled down the other side of the mound, crashed straight into tunnel at the front of the ice house and fell all the way down.

Once the three children had recovered from the shock of encountering this creature, they decided to scarper home before anything else horrid happened. They sincerely hoped the goblin was not dead, but didn't really know what else to do. So, they ran home and were very quiet all through tea. They were very anxious not to tell the grown-ups about the incident and after lots of whispered discussions, they decided to go back the next day with some left-over birthday cake and some sticky plasters, in case the goblin was still alive and had revived.

That was why Joe was now sitting on a rickety seat halfway down a damp, dark tunnel, and wondering what he would see when he reached the bottom.

The six cousin birds perched on a tree nearby.

Chapter 14

The six cousin birds looked on anxiously. Of course, they didn't know any of what had happened yesterday – they could only guess!

Harry gave a little whistle. 'Saints alive, that's SO dangerous!' he murmured to the others on the branch. Who knows what creature is down there? Suppose it's a goblin!'

'Tom and Rose do seem to know what they're doing, though,' replied Sophia quietly.

'Would we do that if it was a goblin?' chirped Bea. 'That's really brave – and why would they be so kind to a dangerous goblin? That one we met last summer was evil – it tried to kill our dear Merry! I mean, why not just leave it there?'

'Well, I suppose Rose, Tom and Joe were brought up to be very kind, weren't they? They are always kind as our parents!' added Alex.

'Well, NOT always!' cheeped Bella. And they all grinned.

They carried on watching anxiously, mesmerized to see what would happen next. Ellie was privately very worried about her daddy – her future daddy. *'What if it is a goblin and it grabs him.'* she thought. *'Supposing he falls off that seat?'*

Tom was shouting down the tunnel. 'Joe are you okay? Is everything alright?' The pulley system was hanging still. It had stopped moving.

Rose called out, 'Joe, rattle the pulley so we know you are okay!' But nothing happened.

She turned to Tom. 'I'm really worried now, Tom. I mean, it's been a good ten minutes. Supposing the goblin attacked him?' They both carried on yelling for Joe, but there was no reply.

Up on their branch, the little birds nudged each other. 'Goblin!' cheeped Sophia quietly. 'Oh no! I knew it! Maybe it's **our** goblin as he was 30 years ago?'

Harry was getting very fidgety. He kept sidestepping along his perch, his head on one side. He wanted to do something for his daddy Joe. But he couldn't think what he could do – he felt so small, so feeble. He was considering flying down the ice house tunnel, but Magic Joe had told them not to be seen. So he stayed hidden, agonising.

Then all of a sudden, the pulley chains rattled. 'Quick, Tom!' Immediately Rose and Tom started hauling on the chains, hand over fist as fast as they could.

Chapter 15

Joe emerged from the tunnel looking pale and shaky. He got off the pulley seat and sat on the edge of the mound with Rose and Tom. He had the lunchbox with him and handed it to Rose.

'Well?' asked Tom. 'You had us worried there, Joey!'

Joe said hoarsely, 'Well, Tom, he's not there. I looked everywhere. I went further in and all around the bottom of the cave. The smell was disgusting. But he just wasn't there. I reckon that he must have recovered from his fall, and felt well enough to climb out. Though heaven knows that would be hard enough – he was only young and small. I guess if you had sharp claws, you could cling on to the brickwork and just climb vertically out. We couldn't do it in a million years, though!'

'Oh! But thank goodness he wasn't dead,' said Tom. 'I hate the idea of that goblin, but it would be awful to have caused his death.'

'Holy horses!' This was Harry.

Down on the ground, Joe slowly uncurled his hand. There sitting in the middle of his palm was a necklace.

Hanging on a slightly rusty silver chain, was a large ruby red stone, oval in shape, set in a rather tarnished silver setting with clasps. It looked old and extremely valuable. The ruby sparkled slightly even in the gloomy winter wood.

'Wow!' breathed Rose. 'Where did you find it, Joe?'

'Crikey!' exclaimed Tom. 'That could be worth a fortune. Awesome!'

'I found it on the floor of the tunnel, my torch picked it up in its beam. But it's not really ours, is it?' said Joe. 'It probably belongs to the goblin and maybe we should leave it here for him. In case he comes looking for it.'

'Yes, but it could just as well have belonged to someone from the big house in the old days,' suggested Rose. 'And anyway, where would a goblin have got something like that in the first place?'

'Yes, but we found it, and well, finders' keepers!' replied Tom.

Now the children were in a moral dilemma. What should they do?

Then they had a bit of an argument about it. They weren't sure if the goblin would return. They certainly didn't want anyone else to find the necklace. But was it right to just take it? Perhaps it should go to a police station? In the end, they decided to take it home and ask the grown-ups if the necklace was valuable and then decide what to do. Rose emptied the crumbly cake bits out of the lunch box, in case the goblin came back. Then they ran off with the ruby necklace in Joe's pocket, out through the woods, glad to be away, at least for today, from the ice house, the wind, the cold and the trees and the very idea of a goblin.

And the little bird cousins sadly reflected that that would be the last they saw of their parents, as children. A sort of gloomy feeling came over them, a feeling of wanting something, yet they weren't sure what.

'Well!' cheeped Alex. 'I would have loved to have had a closer look at that jewel, you know how much I love rocks, jewels and treasures!'

'I know, Alex!' put in Sophia, 'I wish we could have too. What an amazing thing to have found. But oh! I do wish our mummy could have talked to us. I do wish we had been able to show ourselves to them.'

Bella was eyeing up the cake crumbs. 'I'm getting hungry again.' And with that she flew down to the crumbs and started pecking at them with her little beak. The other birds joined her and soon they were all pecking away like the ravenous little birds they were.

'Mm mm, yummy!' they twittered.

'Just exactly what I would have hoped for, made by Rose!' giggled Bea.

Just then, out of nowhere, riding jockey-like on a white seagull, came the very person they most wanted to see.

Chapter 16

Ray the seagull landed on top of the ice house mound and Magic Joe dismounted. The little birds flocked round him cheeping their many questions and hellos at him all at once. They loved Magic Joe so much with his happy smiley face. They blinked and winked at him, and Magic Joe smiled broadly and fondly at them all, stroking their little heads.

They chirped at dear Ray who stood proudly next to Magic Joe. The little birds hopped all around and over him, encouraging him towards the cake crumbs (well, what was left of them).

Magic Joe pulled a wooden carved wand out of his bag and the little bird cousins held their breaths, for they knew it meant some magic was about to occur. He mumbled some words under his breath, and there below them at the base of the ice house mound, the earth started shuffling and parting, creating a small hollow surrounded with large stones. In this hollow there sprang up before them a little fire made from twigs and sticks. It was a perfect open fire with small logs, all contained in the hollow, the flames licking the cold air and any smoke curling straight upwards. For it was cold in those woods, the winter winds howled through the creaking trees, swirling about them all, picking up the dead dry leaves and blowing them about. There was a chill that was not the least bit cheering to them all. All the little birds were feeling gloomy, their feathers ruffling in the winds. They suddenly felt grateful for the light, the warmth and the colours that the golden orange and red flames threw around the small clearing around the ice house. It made them feel immediately cheered in what seemed to them not the least bit cheerful situation. Having Magic Joe and Ray there made them feel instantly relieved.

Magic Joe muttered a few more words and large bowl of warm water appeared nearby and out of his shoulder bag he pulled a wooden cup and he cast a scattering of raisins, dried apple rings, sunflower seeds, and small nut pieces on the ground. The little birds and Ray gathered around and drank and ate ravenously to their hearts' content.

'Ooh, Magic Joe, thank you so much!' they cheeped happily.

So after having eaten and drunk sufficiently they sat near Magic Joe and waited, though they were not sure what they were waiting for.

There was a pause, something expectant in the air.

All of a sudden, they could hear a crackle in the trees and the sound of whooshing. And there, there coming through the woods towards them was a truly frightening sight, the one they least wanted to see. The birds clustered around Magic Joe.

Riding on a large, glossy-feathered jet-black raven, came swooping down the horrid, cruel and disgusting smelling goblin that they remembered so well from Blaxhall woods last summer. It was a truly terrifying sight; the large black bird flew at top speed towards them as if it were a bird of prey. The little birds flocked together, cried out in terror and flew straight up to a tangled thicket of ivy in a nearby group of saplings, where they hid.

The huge handsome raven landed on a boulder and the goblin dismounted sullenly. 'Thank you my dear Rooaz,' said Magic Joe to the raven. 'It was good of you to bring our friend along.'

The shiny black bird bowed its large beaked head to Magic Joe, winked, blinked and then walked sedately off and started pecking at the remains of the bird food with Ray. What a beautiful contrasting pair they looked. Rooaz and Ray. Black and white. Astonishing.

'Holy horses, what's going on?' chirped Harry very quietly. 'I can't stand that goblin – he's no friend of ours!'

'Is this some sort of a trap?' asked Bea nervously. 'I'm frightened. What's Magic Joe doing?'

But they were astounded when the goblin sat quietly but grumpily next to Magic Joe who beckoned the little birds to fly back down again. Which they did nervously, perching at a distance from the goblin, ruffling their feathers. Magic Joe started speaking in his sweet but firm voice.

'Right, my dear little friends. The raven, Rooaz, has kindly brought the goblin to hear what you have to say. There is much you must speak about, I believe. Did you follow my instructions and keep hidden? Did you see what happened? '

The little birds crept a little nearer. 'Yes! blurted out Ellie. 'But my daddy Joe – who was only a little boy – he was in terrible danger. He could have been hurt!'

'Yes, and the goblin, er... a goblin had fallen down this tunnel here, and Joe was lowered in to give him some food and try and rescue him,' tweeted Bella, all in a flurry. 'But he wasn't there.' She eyeballed the goblin suspiciously.

'Yes, and Joe found a beautiful necklace – a lovely ruby and silver necklace. Down at the bottom of the ice hole,' twittered Sophia.

'Rose, Tom and Joe didn't know what to do with it, but in the end, they took it home,' added Bea.

'And we don't know what they did with it after that!' cheeped Alex looking quite vexed.

There was a pause. 'THAT GOBLIN WAS ME,' came a loud growling gruff voice. 'AND THAT NECKLACE WAS MINE.' The goblin had spoken. He looked even more sullen.

And all the cousin birds went silent and stared with shock at the goblin sitting there on the bank.

The bird cousins went silent and stared with shock at the goblin sitting there on the bank.

Chapter 17

Magic Joe spoke. 'I must thank you children for helping me to find out what went on in these woods all those years ago. I wasn't with Rose, Tom and Joe on that fateful day, so I never knew exactly what had happened. Our goblin here has had it in his mind, all that time, to try and find his necklace, but no matter how long he has searched, for however many years, always coming back to these woods, he never could find it. And now he knows why. That has been at the bottom of his misery and meanness for years. He has always hated anyone who is happy and content, because he felt robbed of his own treasure, his own happiness, all those years ago as a young goblin.'

'But where did **he** get the necklace from?' chirped Bea still feeling suspicious.

'Yes. Good question, Bea,' chipped in Alex looking crossly at the goblin. 'You practically destroyed Merry's beautiful woods last year. She, Magic Joe and Ray were all in mortal danger because of you. What have you got to say for yourself?'

The goblin looked sulkily at them all.

Then he started speaking in his gruff ugly voice. It was certainly a different voice from the one they had heard last year when he screamed and yelled at them in the cave. Other than those horrid fearful screams they had not heard him speak at all.

The goblin sat on the stump of a tree with arms folded, looking as if he was defending himself. He looked as hideous as he always had. Red eyes, beaky nose, greasy tuffs of hair, dreadful fang-like teeth and long claw-like finger and toe nails. Still wearing raggedy clothes, he was no nicer to look at. And he smelt disgusting. About the same height as Magic Joe, knee high to the children, he was small, but very ugly and muscly.

But as he spoke, the little cousins began to sense something else about him that they had not ever considered before. A sadness. A sorrow. Something they could relate to.

'That boy made me fall down the tunnel,' the goblin stuttered gruffly, moodily staring at the little birds. (Of course, 'that boy' was Bea and Bella's daddy Tom, but the goblin couldn't know that.) 'I wasn't going to hurt anyone. I was minding my own business looking for mice to eat. I went up the mound and then there were dreadful shouts behind me, and the boy with a big stick, so I made a dash for it and fell down the ice house tunnel. I was only young – I was terrified.' The goblin's eyes narrowed, as if the memory still pained him.

'I don't know how I lost the necklace – I was knocked unconscious. Anything could have happened in the fall – it was such a long way down. I don't remember much, but it was a bad fright.'

Then the goblin explained how his parents had been given that necklace years before by a travelling Romany Gypsy in return for a great favour (although he didn't know what that favour was). His father always wore it with great pride. When their son reached the age of ten, his parents passed it to him. 'They were the only kind goblins in this kingdom,' he said, and for a moment, his angry face softened.

Clearly, the goblin felt it was the greatest honour to have been given such a beautiful and valuable piece of jewellery. And the terrifying fall down the tunnel had made him lose one of the few things that was precious to him. The birds listened in silence, but they were beginning to understand how it felt to him.

The goblin continued his story. 'During the night I came round. I remember the moon was up. I could just see the brickwork but decided to wait for first light to climb out. I could just about grip onto the brickwork with my claws, but it was still a very hard climb. I finally got out about mid-morning. I forgot to check my necklace was still around my neck – I wish I had but I was so tired and cold from being in the ice house all night.'

There was a silence for a moment, but the birds could tell from the goblin's tone of voice that there wasn't a happy ending to his story. Then he told them how when he went back to his cave, something even worse had happened – his father and mother had disappeared. 'They must have gone off to search for me. But they didn't come back. And then I realised I had lost the family necklace! I went back to find it, around the ice house, but I couldn't see it. I couldn't get back down the slippery walls and anyway would not have been able to see anything down there even if I could have. I was going to be in such trouble if my parents knew I had lost it. For the rest of that day, I just hid in the family cave. But my parents didn't come back. I have never seen them since.'

The little birds listened intently, each thinking how they would feel if their parents suddenly went missing.

The goblin was reaching the end of his tale now. 'I was so lonely. Then I felt angry. Then I felt furious that both these precious things had been taken from me – and it wasn't my fault! My family **and** the necklace. And taken by humans too!'

And at that the goblin spat on the ground in disgust (which was truly a revolting thing to do). The little birds looked really shocked.

'Since then, I haven't stopped searching. But I never find them. It isn't **fair**!'

Then the goblin's head bent towards the ground and his eyes filled up.

The six little birds looked at the goblin properly. They were starting to realise why he was so furious with his life and all the other creatures around him. His story went some way to explaining why he felt the need to hurt others. But they also began to feel sorry for him.

'But Magic Joe! For heaven's sake!' chirped Sophia. 'We must sort this out right now! We must go to Rose Cottage and get the necklace back for the goblin, if it's really his!'

'Yes! Somehow, we must explain all that to the children, er, our parents,' cheeped Harry. 'Obviously the goblin shouldn't go around hurting other creatures and being a bad goblin because of this, but I feel a bit sorry for him. He lost everything that day. It must have been awful for him. What can we do? Let's go! Right away! Let's look for it, quickly before Rose, Tom and Joe do something else with it?'

'Oh No! You don't understand!' replied Magic Joe. 'We can't go back in time again now, because the goblin and I arrived in the present! That spell has been broken. It's too late! You travelled into the past as you flew down Half Moon Lane. And then time moved back into the present when the three children ran home. They are no longer at Rose Cottage. They're grown-ups, your parents now, walking in Parham following your 'paper chase' game. Someone else lives here now. And we can't do anything about that.'

Then he sat and thought for a moment. Something like a question mark went across his face. 'Hmmm, though, I wonder? Somehow, we need to find out what happened to that necklace after Joe ran home with it in his pocket. We need to talk to someone who could help us now, but who was there then.' And he stroked his chin, thinking hard.

'Well, it seems pretty obvious to me' piped up Sophia. 'We know exactly who else lived in that house at the same time as our parents when they were young.'

'Who would that be?' asked the goblin gloomily.

And then there was a chorus of the little birds trilling all at once saying rapidly over and over again in tiny excited cheeps: 'Ogo Pogo and Ege Pege! Ogo Pogo and Ege Pege! Ogo Pogo and Ege Pege!'

And there was much fluttering of wings, cheeping, trilling, chirping and general feather ruffling as the little birds chattered together excitedly. 'But where are they?! They set off before us?! What happened?! Why aren't they here?!'

And a load of questions came tumbling, fluttering out of the little birds' beaks, who, in truth, hadn't spared a thought for Ogo Pogo and Ege Pege until now. The cousins had found that tiny note at Parham the day before; they had no idea what had happened to the miniature pixie twins.

Magic Joe put his finger on the side of his nose and winked, pulled his magic wand out of his pocket and muttered a spell under his breath.

Chapter 18

What should it be, but a red squirrel, of all things, who came trotting perkily through the rustling leaves towards them. And there, perched on its back, bumping up and down, were a very grumpy and sleepy looking Ogo Pogo and Ege Pege.

The red squirrel with very grumpy Ogo Pogo and Ege Pege! By Sophia (9 1/2)

'Here we are, Magic Joe!' squeaked the squirrel. 'At your service!' He sat down and the two tiny pixies slid off backwards and did an ungainly roly poly on the ground towards the group, flopping down on the cold earth. They picked themselves up and brushed themselves off.

'Well, really!' said Ogo Pogo in his squeaky grumpy voice, hands on hips. 'First you bump us all the way to this wood and then having got us nice and warm and cosy and asleep, you suddenly wake us up and say it's time to go! It's NOT funny!'

Ogo and Ege looked crossly at all the little birds who were twittering and chuckling with glee at seeing their dear tiny crosspatch friends again.

'Yes!' squeaked Ege. 'You should try riding on the back of a squirrel all that way from Parham. it's no fun. It took hours and hours! Why, Magic Joe, couldn't you have just waved your wand and got us here with your magic without any fuss? It's a mystery. We were on the road till the early hours this morning. And then! Then! We had to sleep in this squirrel's dray which was really prickly, full of twigs and pieces of bark, not a bit like our cosy match box.'

And Ege sat down with a bump and folded his arms crossly.

Then Ogo and Ege looked about them and saw the goblin sitting sullenly apart from the rest of the group. They moved closer together and tried their very best to look fierce. They saw the six little birds who were twittering and flying around them, and began to wonder what they were doing there.

Magic Joe cleared his throat, trying not to laugh. 'Well, dear Ogo and Ege! So sorry for your mode of transport, though I do think you might spare a thought for my friend Nutters, he had to run a long way and for many hours to get here. Thank you, dear squirrel, and for the loan of your nest for the weary travellers! As to why you were brought here more slowly, Ogo and Ege, it was because I couldn't quite trust you to keep quiet and just observe what was going on earlier. Also, I needed you to leave that note in Parham for the children, who are here now in the form of these young stonechat birds. You had a very important part to play you know.'

At that the two miniature pixies perked up with self-importance, and looked a little more pleased about life. They were also delighted to see their dear friends, the cousins, even if they were a flock of small birds, now flying around Ogo Pogo and Ege Pege in a great flutter of wings and calls of welcome.

So then Magic Joe told Ogo Pogo and Ege Pege the whole story from beginning to end, leaving out no details.

'So that's it. And now we ask you – do you know anything about the necklace and what happened to it

after it went back in Joe's pocket to Rose Cottage?'
Magic Joe concentrated on the miniature pair.

The two pixies looked at each other.

'Well, that's right, Magic Joe,' squeaked Ogo Pogo. 'We
were there when the children came running in with the
necklace. They showed it to their father, who knew
about those sorts of things. They didn't mention
anything about a goblin, of course. Their father said he
thought it was just a bit of costume jewellery, used by
people sometimes to look like the real thing when they
were going out for a posh evening.'

'Well! That's NOT true for a start!' complained the
goblin moodily.

'Then what happened?' asked Magic Joe.

'The next day,' squeaked Ege Pege, 'After giving it a
good polish up, Rose, Tom and Joe put the necklace on
their FOR SALE table outside the house gate. They
put a price tag of £3.00 on it which Ogo and I thought
was quite a bit of money – £1 each!'

Then Ogo Pogo continued in his squeaky voice. 'But you
know, it was winter, it was dark by late afternoon, and
well, after that, we don't know what happened. The
next day, the children came running into the house
telling us that the necklace had gone but no money had
been left in the jam jar. They were really upset. Of

course, they told us they thought someone must had taken it. Though they didn't want to mention a goblin for fear of the whole story coming out.'

'Well, I didn't take it,' said the goblin gruffly. 'Though I wish I had known about it being on the For SALE table, because I certainly WOULD have taken it!'

The assembled company looked around at each other with question marks in their eyes.

'Who would do such a thing?' chirped Ellie. 'That's not nice at all!'

'Well, perhaps it was just a greedy person without any thoughts of anyone else,' answered Bella.

There was a long silence as they all waited, thinking what on earth they could do. Everyone seemed mesmerised by the embers and flames in the little fire and warmed themselves as they thought.

Finally, there was a little cough as one of the creatures cleared his throat. And Rooaz the raven, who until then had been listening intently with his head on one side, hopped up into the middle of the group. Everyone cleared a space and looked at him carefully. His handsome face his great beak and shiny black coat was really impressive. He seemed to grow slightly in stature as he stood up straight to speak.

Clearing his throat, Rooaz began in a low, cawing voice.

Rooaz the raven. By Sophia (9 ¾)

Chapter 19

'Ah hem!' Rooaz croaked. 'I believe I know what happened to it. You see we birds in the crow family have very sharp eyes. I myself wouldn't mind such a treasure if I came across it, not that I would lower myself to steal it. But there has long been a story connected with a piece of jewellery such as the one described today. And there are rumours that we do have some serious thieves in the bird kingdom.' He bowed his head and thought for a moment. Then taking a deep breath he crowed, 'It is with much regret that I have to tell you that I believe a magpie stole it.'

'What?!' twittered all the little cousin birds at once. 'How do you know?' What do you know?'

'Well,' continued Rooaz steadily with his head turning this way and that so that he could fix them all with his beady eyes. 'My parents told me the tale when I was a chick, and it connects exactly to the circumstances here. You see, I too grew up in these woods and we all knew the story as youngsters. It became folklore. We have large families, we ravens. A group of us together is known as 'an unkindness' by the humans. It's a strange name don't you think? Anyway, we live in the tops of the trees in our nests, and have very sharp eyes. There's not much that goes on that we don't know about.'

'We were told that the magpie stole the necklace from the FOR SALE table and flew away to another area where he was not known. Magpies have an eye for glittery things and some say they will take them to decorate their nests to attract a female mate. Their nick names are not 'thieving magpies' for nothing. They are very intelligent birds, in fact, nearly the most intelligent creatures on earth (next to ravens of course).' At that, Rooaz winked. 'And they live high up in the trees, like us. Anyway, that's what I was told happened. Though of course, it was a long time ago.'

The magpie with the ruby necklace

Magic Joe looked sternly at the raven. 'Are you sure about this, Rooaz?' he asked. 'That's quite a serious accusation to make against a fellow bird.'

'I am as sure as I can be,' replied the raven. I have many relatives who could vouch for this story.'

'But do you know where he went?' chirped Bea in great consternation. 'We need to find him if we can!' All the little birds twittered in great excitement.

'Well, yes I do as a matter of fact,' croaked Rooaz calmly. 'You see, one day my uncle came home from an expedition further afield near a river. He had gone there for a spectacular gathering of ravens. They were holding an important conference. My uncle told us that while he was there, he had come across a pair of magpies who had boasted about their great wealth. They said they were the owners of a beautiful necklace they had 'found' in Redgrave Tangle Wood. But the magpies said they had escaped to the country round a great river, to make a new life. Gosh, well this must have been about 30 years ago. Since then, of course, I have no idea what happened to them.' Rooaz had a faraway look with his beady eye, as if he was trying to remember something else.

'Wow!' chirped Alex excitedly. 'Which river was it, where was the meeting, can we go there to look for the nest?'

'Do you know where it is, Rooaz?' cheeped Bea.

'Did anyone ever tell you about it?' chirped Harry.

'Well, yes!' cawed Rooaz. I go there every summer for a change of air. All my family go there in the spring to make nests in the cliff sides, lay eggs and hatch our chicks. It's a beautiful woodland near a river about 35 miles south east from here, as the crow flies! The river is called the river Orwell and the woodland is known as Home Wood. It's a beautiful part of Suffolk, of course – the lovely stretch of water and river beach there became known as "Long Reach". It's quite near the sea too and not far from the seaside town called Felixstowe.'

A sort of dawning sensation came over all the small cousin birds. They knew instinctively where this was leading to. Harry and Ellie started getting excited. Their energy was rising and they felt they knew what was coming. They stretched their wings, paced back and forth on the branch and ruffled their feathers, fixing the raven with their blinking eyes.

Ellie and Harry started trilling in a chorus, excitedly, 'We know it! Of course! Of course! It's just near our home!'

Alex slowed down the conversation and twittered. 'But why didn't you get the necklace before, years ago?' Alex was still very interested in the value of it. 'If you all knew about it, why didn't you get it?'

'Well, we don't steal things like magpies do. We're not thieves and robbers,' replied Rooaz, shaking his head. 'So we never really bothered, we never thought about it. What would we do with a necklace!?'

The goblin moodily grumbled and groaned in his coarse voice. 'To think I've been looking all these years, I've searched all the woods in Suffolk, including those woods. To think that all along, the necklace was right under my nose… or rather… right above my head!'

'Well! Come on then!' trilled Sophia. 'Let's go! Let's get on with it right now! Let's go and find the necklace for the goblin and then we can all go home!' She was getting impatient and fed up with being in these dark cold windy woods.

But just as she had chirped those words her voice trailed off. She suddenly yawned, and so did all the other little birds – they had that funny, 'must go to sleep' feeling again. It came upon them so suddenly. They felt they needed to crowd together on a branch for warmth.

Magic Joe could see what was happening. It was time for them to roost. A moody darkness was taking over Tangle Woods. The wind had dropped. Dusk was falling, there was no chance of doing any more or going anywhere else today. The light drained away rapidly. It had been a long day with much to adjust to for all the assembled company. Even the goblin was feeling weary.

Magic Joe brought his magic wand out of his shoulder bag and said these charmed words:

'Birds of the day, creatures of the night,

It's time for you to cease your flight.

Be warm and safe, sleep until dawn,

Be quiet and still until the morn.

Now is the time, renewed by sun,

To count our blessings one by one.'

Ogo Pogo and Ege Pege settled back by the embers of the fire in a nest of dry autumn leaves that the squirrel, Nutters, had been collecting, mainly for himself! They covered themselves with the leaves and were soon feeling warm and sleepy. Nutters scampered away into another hollow of a tree trunk, and curled up there. Ray and Rooaz flew up into a branch of a large tree, high up where they could keep an eye on the little cousin birds.

Magic Joe sat by the warming fire and stared into the red and amber crackling flames. A crescent moon pale and yellow had risen above the trees. Pulling his cloak around him, he had a far-away look and a twinkle in his eyes. He was remembering happy times as a young pixie in these woods, reliving magical times of his youth, playing with his dear sister Merry and the children Rose, Tom and Joe. So many years ago, now. He pulled a small wooden penny whistle out of his shoulder bag and started playing it. It wasn't a particularly merry tune, but a slow sweet melody. The animals all relished the warmth of the fire and the beauty of the music. Ray, Rooaz, Ogo Pogo, Ege Pege, Nutters and the small stonechats listened, imagining they were living the stories in Magic Joe's memory of long-ago times. They imagined they could see white sugar mice, gingerbread men and calling birds flying through the trees.

Alex, Sophia, Bea, Harry, Bella and Ellie were also recollecting another time (in another story) when dear Magic Merry had given them tea in Blaxhall woods, along with her two dear animal friends, Hedgy and Nibbler. Then they had all danced and sung around a fire, quite similar to this one. Warm comforting memories. Bea wished Magic Merry was here now.

One by one the six little cousin birds put their heads under their wing and dropped off into a deep sleep. They felt safe and warm. They dreamed of three smiling children who lived in a thatched cottage nearby.

In the hollow of a tree, set apart, the goblin curled up. He was cold, isolated and felt bleak. His memories were only of loss, of loneliness, unhappiness and sorrow. But he did not flinch at the sound of the music, he let it wash over him and without realising it he felt a little soothed. Not knowing why, he began to feel just a little better in his spirits as a spark of something called 'hope' was ignited in his heart. He drifted into a restless sleep.

Tangle Wood at night.

Chapter 20

Early morning dawned bright and quiet. As the sky brightened, a low watery sun broke through the silhouetted trees in rays of pure gold. A hoar frost lay upon the ground, crisp white and sparkling. In the wood the shadows were violet and rich mossy green. Overhead the frosted branches made a silvery pattern against the brilliant blue of the clear, cloudless sky. Sunlight filtered into the clearing where the little group sat, melting the crisp frozen skeleton leaves. The wind, the 'beast from the east', had miraculously dropped. It was one of those late December/January mornings that tries to trick you into believing that spring is only round the corner, just a little way off.

Alex was the first stonechat to open his little beady eye. He started chattering and whistling before he knew it – a sharp loud call that sounded like two stones being banged together. He couldn't help himself and was in full song as the others stirred and blinked.

'Oi, Alex,' grumbled Sophia, opening one eye, 'give it a rest! That's a bit much first thing in the morning!'

'I can't stop it,' Alex managed in the middle of a loud cheep.

Next thing, all the little cousin birds were stirring and had started joining Alex in a chirping and cheeping that seemed to make them feel alive and happy for no particular reason. Even Sophia, who couldn't help herself. They were sidestepping right and left along the branch as they sang. They loved the glory of the morning, so bright, so clean and untroubled.

Magic Joe sat up and rubbed his eyes. He poked at the embers of the fire with a nearby stick and it sprang to life. Ray and Rooaz also opened an eye each and looked down at the little birds slightly grumpily. 'Bit early for this, wouldn't you say, Rooaz?' squawked Ray.

But there was no stopping them and soon the two large birds were joining in with their caws and seagull cries as well.

A nearby red-breasted Robin eyeballed them all from a nearby tree. 'Hey, shush you lot!' he chirped in a sharp little voice. But then to his dismay, he found that he couldn't help but do the same. A blackbird joined in too, with its beautiful shrill whistling call. Soon all of Tangle Wood was alive with other small birds cheeping and trilling.

'Look what you started!' chuckled Sophia. 'Really, Alex!'

Ogo Pogo and Ege Pege stopped their tiny snoring, grumbled in high squeaky voices about being disturbed, and sat up. Their swirls of white hair were sticking up in all directions and they had leaves clinging to them. They looked like a couple of tiny wild woodland scarecrows. Seeing them just made the little cousin birds twitter even more loudly. Nutters the squirrel scampered over, sat up by the warm fire and started cleaning his face and whiskers with his front paws, his nose twitching.

The goblin lumbered over sheepishly and sat on a boulder at a distance saying nothing. He looked a little more refreshed for his sleep. Bea observed this and being perceptive, wondered why he seemed a little calmer than he had yesterday. She watched the goblin closely and saw a difference in him that she couldn't name, but it felt good.

Magic Joe produced some amazing-looking cake from his shoulder bag. He seemed always to have an endless supply of food on him. This time it was acorn cake with dried fruit and hazelnuts in it.

He sprinkled some of the cake on the ground around the fire for the birds and magically refilled the wooden bowl with warm water. The birds all fell on the food and drink with gusto. Giving Ogo, Ege and the goblin pieces of scrumptious cake and drinks from walnut shells, he began talking.

'Now then, everyone,' he said. 'It's time to get over to Home Wood. We need to help the goblin resolve this issue and as soon as possible. I think, at last, we know why he has been such a wicked goblin. He lost everything and he feels very aggrieved and lonely because of it. He took it out on all of us in a cruel and unfeeling way, and for that we would want him to say sorry and ask forgiveness, one day. You little birds did very well to help us uncover the mystery which Merry and I couldn't work out back at Blaxhall Woods. But now we need to try and put this back together for him and at least recover something that was rightfully his, if we can. Perhaps we will never know what happened to your parents, goblin, but at least this is a start.'

Everyone nodded enthusiastically in agreement. The little cousins couldn't wait to get out into the open skies again and to be near their beloved sea and river. Ray and Rooaz, so strong and beautiful, looked ready for anything. They all listened intently with their heads on one side.

'So here is the plan. We need to fly together to the area of woodland around the river shore. We will have to try and track down a group of magpies, perhaps asking other birds for information as we go. It will not be easy. Of all the creatures in the woods, magpies are the least friendly to other birds. They can be unkind to smaller birds and often steal another bird's nest and lay their eggs in it. But do not be deceived, they are very intelligent and will watch who comes and goes. They sometimes hold big meetings, just like our friends the crows. There may be many of them together there.'

'You will be able to tell a magpie. It is very striking with its black and white plumage, and very long green iridescent indigo tail which shimmers in the sunlight. You will recognise it by its call is which is 'mag, mag, mag!'

Ray and Rooaz tried not to feel offended at the mention of how handsome the magpie is.

'So,' continued Magic Joe, 'I suggest we go to the edge of the wood and then make a plan when we get there and can see the lay of the land. It is quite a journey from here and we need to set off before any wind gets up again.'

Ogo Pogo chimed up in his tiny squeaky voice. 'I beg your pardon, Magic Joe, but we do hope you are not thinking of sending us on that long journey riding on the back of Nutters again? No offence, Nutters, but you are a bumpy ride.'

Magic Joe stifled a giggle and spoke directly to the squirrel. 'Dear Nutters, you have been of great service to us these last two days. But now I suggest you make your way back at Parham and your family.'

Nutters bowed his head and said in a serious and squeaky little voice, 'it has been my pleasure and my honour, Magic Joe, and if you ever need any more help, you only have to ask.' Without further ado, he turned about and scampered away through the woods, his red tail flying behind him.

'And as for the rest of us... this is how we shall travel.'

And pulling out his magic wand, Magic Joe outlined his travelling plans, drawing maps in the soil.

Chapter 21

The golden sun shone in a cloudless azure blue sky. Frosty glitter was below them, dusting the tree tops and making white criss-cross patterns on the fields below. Rays of sunshine slanted across as the group flew towards the coast. It was a totally different journey from that of yesterday morning. Everyone loved it apart from the goblin, who was incapable of liking anything, it seemed.

Riding at the front of the group was the seagull Ray, ridden by Magic Joe who was sandwiched between Ogo Pogo and Ege Pege. The two tiny pixies were holding on for dear life trying not to slide off the shiny seagull feathers or be blown away by the wind. Magic Joe kept catching hold of Ogo Pogo's breeches in front of him, and Ege Pege behind was gripping tightly to Magic Joe's belt.

Behind the bright white seagull came the six little stonechat bird cousins, flying in a group taking it in turns to lead or fly at the rear. They all flapped their little wings quickly to keep up with Magic Joe and Ray.

Someway behind them all came the goblin riding on the glossy black raven, Rooaz.

'I do hate that goblin being behind us like that!' chirped Bella breathlessly, peering back over her shoulder. 'I feel as if I'm being chased by a baddy in a film.'

'Well, we'd better keep up with Magic Joe then!' tweeted back Sophia. They all flapped their wings a bit harder.

But on the whole, the little birds were having a wonderful flight. There was no head wind to speak of, as they were travelling pretty much due south. Any wind there was just pushed them along. It was delightful. There is such a feeling of freedom in flying as a bird – just the breeze in your feathers, peace and quiet and the sunshine around you. A bit like sailing on a vast river, but without the clutter of a boat. And of course, the views were spectacular. Because they were taking the most direct route 'as the crow flies', it wasn't a bit like having to drive in cars on roads. They were flying across country, zooming over woodland, fields and farms. Small rooftops glistened and shimmered in the icy sunshine below them. They swooped and glided smoothly along without event, occasionally opening their beaks to grab a passing flying insect as they went.

After about an hour, Ray and Magic Joe glided down to the edge of a small wood next to the river Gipping. They had reached a pretty village called Bramford on the outskirts of Ipswich. As they descended, they glided round the tall spire of a church in a spiral. A footpath and some woodland ran along the side of the river. Ray landed on the bank of the river next to the bridge over it. Magic Joe dismounted and Ray waddled down to the river edge and had a good drink. The other little birds, Rooaz and the goblin followed suit. Ogo and Ege tumbled off Ray and ran around the little beach to stretch their legs and get warm. Aware that they did not want to be seen, the goblin and Magic Joe ducked underneath the arch of the bridge, sheltering inside the tunnel on a dry bank of the cold running water. Magic Joe fed them all again from the cake supplies in his shoulder bag.

Chapter 22

As they were all eating hungrily, an elderly, stooped woman walked across the bridge nearby. She wore a tweed jacket and matching skirt, woolly beige tightsand walking boots, and had a head scarf tied under her chin. She was off to get her newspaper from the village shop. She had a stout walking stick. Lumbering alongside her was a fat, furry yellow Labrador. He was not on the lead. The woman was quite a bit ahead of her dog. Suddenly the hairy dog started dribbling, panting and growling – he could smell the goblin's vile stink. The dog panted as his tongue lolled out of his mouth, then he spotted the two tiny pixies, Ogo and Ege. Teeth bared and growling, he leapt down the bank. The birds let out a cry of alarm and flew quickly out of danger to the branch of a nearby tree.

'Saints alive!' chirped Harry in alarm, 'Look! That dog is after Ogo and Ege!'

All the little birds started chirruping and cheeping at the top of their voices. Their alarm calls were very shrill. Ray and Rooaz looked on, confused – being much higher at the tree top, they couldn't quite see what all the commotion was.

'Quick! Do something!' cried Alex.

In a flash the six birds flew round and round the dog's head, trying to put him off the scent of the two pixies. They fluttered in every direction, squawking and chattering their alarm call. Ray and Rooaz swooped to join them and soon there were some dreadful alarm cries.

But still the dog snapped its jaws and growled, head down, trying to get at the two tiny pixies who were dancing this way and that as best they could, trying to dodge being caught. Being the size of a little finger had its advantages and the two sprightly pixies were good at springing clear of the old dog, even though they were so elderly themselves. They yelled and shouted at the dog in their fiercest squeaky voices. To the dog they looked like two tiny tasty mice or birds. However, the two of them were getting tired and they couldn't keep it up much longer. It looked as if any minute they would be snapped up by the dog's huge teeth. There was such a hullabaloo with, in addition, the birds' alarm calls: seagull, raven, stonechats all crying out.

'Help!' squealed Ogo Pogo in shrill alarm. 'Save us!'

'Argh!' yelled Ege Pege at the top of his tiny voice. He tripped backwards over a stone and lay flattened on the shingle.

The dog's slobbering tongue, smelly breath and sharp teeth closed in on Ege Pege's little body.

The dog started panting and growling.

Chapter 23

Magic Joe could see what was going on from under the bridge and quickly pulled his magic wand out of his shoulder bag.

But then suddenly, a very wonderful thing happened. The goblin, in double quick time, charged out from under the bridge, and threw a large piece of Magic Joe's cake further away, along the riverbank, for the dog to fetch. The dog, momentarily distracted, twisted his head away from Ege and started going for the cake (Labradors are such greedy dogs!). Quick as a flash, the goblin scooped up Ogo Pogo and Ege Pege in both muscly hands, darted back to Magic Joe and dropped the two terrified squealing pixies into the shoulder bag. Ogo and Ege weren't sure who they were most frightened of, the dog or the goblin!

The woman, who had heard the terrible commotion, had turned and was striding back for the dog. The birds all flew straight up into the nearest branch. 'Come along, George!' she called angrily in a loud horsy voice, brandishing her walking stick at the dog. 'What are you doing? Leave those poor hungry birds alone!' She grabbed the dog, clipped his lead onto his collar and pulled him away from the cake. 'And that's definitely NOT your breakfast either!' She strode off, pulling at the snarling dog, muttering to herself, 'Well really! Of all the things! Six stonechats, a raven and a seagull all in one place, I've never seen anything like it! Wait till I tell Mr Ink at the Newsagents!' The dog sulkily followed her.

Everyone was shaky after that incident. Magic Joe was annoyed with himself for not having the foresight to see something like this could happen. He was also cross that he didn't take better care of Ogo and Ege and act quicker. The little group gathered under the bridge, the cousins all twittering at once

'Holy Moses!' shivered Harry, 'that was a close shave!'

'Are you okay, Ogo and Ege?' chirped Bea.

No sound came from inside of Magic Joe's shoulder bag.

'That was very brave of you, goblin!' cheeped Alex in admiration.

The little birds gathered round the goblin and looked at him. 'Thank you! That was so quick thinking of you, it was such a clever thing to do!' chirped Sophia with genuine respect.

'You saved their lives!' cheeped Bella.

Ogo Pogo and Ege Pege poked their heads out of the top of Magic Joe's bag and managed wan small smiles.

Something really good had come of it. This was the very first time for many, many years that the goblin had done something unselfish and brave. After all, he had endangered his own life in saving the two miniature pixies.

 And as they all looked at him, a strange thing happened. His eyes, which had always been angry, frightening and an ugly red colour, turned a pleasant grey and the children could see the beginnings of a twinkle in them. His revolting black teeth became more apparent as he curled his lips up in the start of a real smile.

All the little birds started laughing and giggling in their bird voices with relief, which made the goblin smile his gruesome smile even more.

'I think it's time you had a name, goblin. You would never tell us what it is.' said Magic Joe, his head on one side.' Would you like us to give you a new name? Or have you got a name already?'

'Well,' replied the goblin in his ugly gruff voice. 'I did have a name, but I have such sad memories of it and haven't used it since, well, since my parents left me.'

'What was your name? asked Magic Joe gently.

'It was Devlin,' replied the goblin slowly.' But I haven't heard that name for so many years. I'm not sure I feel like Devlin anymore. I lost my feeling for it the day my parents disappeared.'

'Would you like us to call you that?' asked Magic Joe kindly. 'Or would you like us to give you a new name?'

The goblin stared across the river and thought for many moments. Eventually he replied.

'I think I would like a new name, so that I can make a new beginning.'

And that was the best news the cousins had heard for ages.

Magic Joe pulled out his magic wand. He looked at the goblin and pointed the wand over his head circling three times in each direction. Everyone became very still. Drawing a circle in the sand around the goblin he pointed his wand in the four compass point directions saying these words:

'Spirit of the North -power of Winter, Spirit of the East- power of Spring

Spirit of the South- power of Summer, Spirit of the West – power of Autumn

Take this creature and turn him round,

Give him the name so that he can be found.

Give him strength to turn to the light,

Fight for good and all that is right.

*Goblin we give you the name **Druego The Strong.***

We welcome you.'

And then all the birds, Ogo and Ege who were watching from the safety of Magic Joe's shoulder bag, and the goblin too, uttered the word 'Druego' a few times as if they were trying it on for size. It was a strange little chorus coming from all the birds' chattering, squeaks from Ogo and Ege and grunts from the newly named goblin. But a strange feeling of peace descended on them all as they spoke it. And then they all joined in with the last line of the magic spell, that they knew so well.

'Now is the time, renewed by sun, to count our blessings one by one.'

There was the incredible Orwell Bridge spanning the river.

Chapter 24

After a little while, the group took off again and flew up high out of sight of anyone who might glance to the sky. A pixie and goblin flying on the top of a seagull and a raven would no doubt attract unwanted attention! Everyone was feeling more cautious – they certainly did not want any more incidents.

Harry began to concentrate on the landscape below. A bird's eye view is full of information! He felt like he was zooming in on Google Earth and began to recognise some of the landmarks. *'Wow!'* he thought to himself. *'I think we're flying over the Orwell Bridge! Awesome!'* And sure enough, there was that incredible bowed bridge supported on vast pillars spanning the river. He could see Ipswich docks and town on one side of the bridge, woods and countryside on the other. They flew high, directly across the top of the bridge crossing over the hundreds of cars and lorries trundling along it in both directions. They followed the broad river as it snaked away from Ipswich town, flying right along the middle of it. The tide was out and Bea could see the river bed either side full of wading birds pecking at chewy morsels in the mud. *'Ew'* thought Bea giggling to herself. *'I'm glad I'm not a wader!'* There was a small marina on the right-hand side, boat masts all standing vertically in a group. *'Amazing!'* thought Harry. *'We're nearly at our house!'*

And at last, they arrived at their destination. They all landed on the river shore. The children all recognised immediately the lovely grassy bank and river beyond, where they often came for picnics and adventures with the grown-ups. Ogo and Ege climbed out of Magic Joe's shoulder bag, and jumped down onto the beach. They were relieved to be back on land. Looking at the river there were woods to the right. To the left, a sandy muddy beach, woods beyond and the big cranes of Felixstowe Port in the distance. Ellie and Harry felt they were on home turf.

'Right, now then,' said Magic Joe. 'Here is the plan. We need to split up and search the tree tops around here. Rooaz, do you have any idea whereabouts you think your uncle saw the magpies and their nests?'

'Not really,' said Rooaz apologetically.

'It doesn't matter, Rooaz,' said Magic Joe kindly. 'You little stone chats: you will fly off in twos and circle round the tops of the trees. Obviously with the river in the West, we only have three directions to search – North, East and South. Bea and Harry, you two fly above the trees through the woods going back towards the Orwell Bridge. Sophia and Bella, you fly high inland towards the East. Alex and Ellie, you go South searching the trees along the river towards the sea. Druego and I will fill in the areas in between on Ray and Rooaz, and try looking a little further away and along the back of the fields behind. Ogo Pogo and Ege Pege, you will choose two of the little bird cousins to ride on. You have sharp little eyes and we need you to help.'

'Right oh!' squeaked Ogo excitedly. To be honest, he and Ege were fed up with riding in Magic Joe's shoulder bag – interesting as it was – because they couldn't see anything from there and felt they were missing all the sights. Besides, they wanted to be useful again.

Ege clambered onto the back of Alex who smiled at him happily and Ogo climbed onto the back of Harry. All boys together! Both the boys were thrilled to have such an important passenger each!

'Hold on tightly, won't you!' Harry tweeted with concern in his voice.

'You are all looking for a group of nests that are high up in the canopies of the woodlands,' continued Magic Joe. 'When you find some, just fly over the tops and see if you can spot anything shiny in them. Be very careful not to annoy any resident magpies. They are not overly friendly and could easily try and frighten you off, if they think you are spying. In addition, if you do find something, you are to give your loudest alarm cry and one of us will hear you and come. Do not try and pick anything up with your beak or carry anything, you never know if the jewel is enchanted carrying a magic spell, and secondly you might drop it.'

'But Magic Joe,' chirped Sophia. 'You might not hear our whistle? We can't sing that loudly!'

Magic Joe pulled his magic wand out of his shoulder bag and circled it three times in each direction over the assembled group, muttering some words.

'Now try!' he smiled.

The birds all gave the most incredibly loud alarm shrieks, and whistles. Ogo Pogo and Ege Pege found they had very loud squeaky high-pitched voices.

'Ha! ha! That's awesome!' cheeped Sophia, whose voice had the most piercing whistle any of them had ever heard. They all started laughing and chirping all at once. The racket was dreadful!

Magic Joe shook his head and stuffed his fingers in his ears. 'Right oh! Only use that whistle when you absolutely have to!'

So off they flew in the directions they had been told.

Down on Nacton Foreshore.

Chapter 25

Bea and Harry (with Ogo Pogo on his back) flew over the tops of the thick woodland either side of an overgrown muddy path, that led along the riverside towards the Orwell Bridge. Looking down, Harry could clearly see the rickety walkway that straddled the path. He remembered those rotten planks from great walks with his family. He gestured to Bea to look, as they flew over an ancient old oak tree lying on its side. It was totally hollowed out. It looked like a truly gruesome monster all gnarled up, but he had loved climbing over, in and around it with Ellie and his cousins when they visited.

They kept going upwards towards the tree tops.

Suddenly there was a yelp from Ogo Pogo: 'Look!' He pointed down at a group of rough twiggy looking nests at the top of some trees. They seemed just like the nests that Magic Joe had mentioned to look for. Bea and Harry flew higher to get a good look inside them.

'In there!' squawked Ogo in his loudest tiny voice Bea and Harry couldn't believe their eyes when they noticed some things glittering in one of them.

'Harry!' Bea chirped quietly, 'Look! Is that what I think it is?'

Bea flew nearer and peered inside the nest. Together they could make out some shiny jewel-like objects. One of them was ruby red, glittering and attached to a silver neck chain. Forgetting what Magic Joe had said about not touching anything, Bea, in an instant, dived straight into the nest and picked up the necklace in her beak.

'No, Bea, **stop! Don't** touch it!' squawked Ogo Pogo. But it was too late, Bea had flown up out of the nest with the necklace.

In an instant seven angry magpies appeared from nowhere. Coming from every direction they closed in towards the two cousins screeching at them with their machine-gun-like squawks.

'Wok Wok Wok Wokawok!' they screamed.

Flashing black and white, they were striking and terrifying to Bea and Harry who were such small dull-looking birds by comparison. Ogo Pogo clung on tightly to Harry, lying close to his neck, hoping not to get noticed. The seven fearsome creatures surrounded them, getting ever closer. Black and white wing feathers spanning outwards, screeching as they flew. 'Oi! Oi!,' they cried. 'Robbers! Thieves! Ours! Ours!'

Harry screeched back with vigour, 'No! It's NOT yours! Get away get away!' But one of the magpies had closed in on Harry and took a swipe at him with a wing.

'Look out!' squealed Ogo. Harry was put off balance for a moment and he nearly fell to the ground. But Ogo bravely shouted at the magpie while Harry righted himself, swooped under the bigger bird and dived into a thicket of small branches. The magpie followed but couldn't get inside. Ogo, lying flat on Harry's back clung on for dear life. The others were closing in, splitting into two groups; four of them chasing Bea who was ducking and diving, swerving in and out of the trees, the necklace hanging from her beak.

One magpie closed in on Bea, took a stab at her with its sharp beak and grabbed some of her tail feathers. 'Ours! Ours!' it screamed.

Bea faltered for a moment losing forwards momentum, then the tail feather came out. Released, she rolled over and pivoted round so she was behind the magpie. Swooping away behind, she dived under the other three approaching magpies and zoomed towards Harry. Holding on tightly to the necklace in her beak, she flew with all her might.

Harry suddenly remembered what to do! He let out the most enormous alarm call. It was shrill, and distinct. He yelled out again. Ogo Pogo joined him with his own high-pitched squawk. Together they pierced through the sounds of everything around them. Even the angry attacking magpies were momentarily silenced by it.

Then they were all off again. Together Bea and Harry dodged, diving in and out between the naked branches of the thickest trees, swooping under and over twigs and sprigs. This annoyed the magpies who, while chasing, were too big to exactly follow the two small birds, who were so nimble. They momentarily lost sight of their prey.

Harry and Bea had reached the fallen old gnarled oak tree that they knew from family picnics. 'Quick! Bea, in here!' Harry, with Ogo Pogo clinging on for dear life, swooped inside the cavity of the old horizontal tree and hid himself in one of the darker gnarled areas inside. Bea followed and hooked the necklace over a knob protruding inside a cavity of the monster like tree. It was quite well hidden and so were they. All around them outside the tree they could hear the machine-like 'Wok! Wok a Wok!' of the confused magpies.

'Saints preserve us!' cheeped Harry, breathing heavily.

'We need a plan!' whispered Bea. 'We'll be dead meat if we stay in here too long!'

'But the necklace could stay here,' muttered Harry. 'They'd never find it!'

'I'll stay in here with it,' whispered Ogo Pogo bravely. 'They won't find it if they try, because I'll be hiding it from view. And I'm ready for them!' He picked up a stick which was really just a large twig, looking like a tiny fierce warrior, ready to swipe at anything that tried to approach him.

'Okay, if you're sure, Ogo! chirped Bea quietly. 'That's very brave of you. Harry and I will lure the Magpies away from here. If we fly towards where the others were, towards the beach where we all started, someone else might come to help us. We certainly don't want to draw all the birds here where the jewel is hidden,' she added sensibly.

'Yes, we can surprise the magpies if we swoop out of nowhere suddenly. Split up and fly parallel but apart towards the beach,' whispered Harry.

But it was nearly too late to carry on discussing a plan. Harry, peering out of one end, could see one of the magpies swooping down towards their hiding place.

'Magpies! Quick Bea, this way!' he trilled. 'Dear Ogo, we PROMISE we'll come back for you! Don't go anywhere, will you!'

The two of them zoomed out of the other end of the fallen tree and shot upwards into the canopy above. The chase was back on again.

And Ogo Pogo, taking a deep breath in that dark cave like place, felt immediately terrified. He stood guard in front of the necklace and braced himself.

The Magpies swooped down on Bea, Harry and Ogo Pogo.

By Ellie (6)

Chapter 26

Meanwhile, Sophia and Bella had heard Harry and Ogo Pogo's alarm cries. They instantly turned round and started swooping back towards where they thought the sound had come from. But unwittingly they were flying straight towards Harry and Bea who were being closely pursued by the seven magpies. They were about to fly into real danger! Without hesitating, Bella and Sophia let out their enormously loud alarm calls. 'Help! Help!' they squawked.

Likewise, Alex and Ellie had heard the alarm and were flying back towards the beach. It was not far away, but they could see a group of birds ahead, four small ones and seven black and white ones chasing them. Alex's heart gave a thud. *'Oh no!'* he thought. *'The others are under attack from the magpies!'* He and Ellie also let out the alarm calls as they dived into the muddle of birds. They tried their best to confuse and disorientate the magpies.

'Hold on tightly, Ege!' trilled Alex to the tiny pixie riding on his back. 'Hang on for dear life!'

There was an immensely loud noise going on – all the birds together making a fearful cacophony of squawks, trills, cheeps and alarm calls. Flashes of black and white, orange, and brown were everywhere. There was total chaos as the six little stonechats were being pushed jostled and dived at by the swift and aggressive magpies with their rat-a-tat alarm calls. The little birds were quick and they swooped and ducked as best they could. It was true that the magpies were bewildered by the sudden number of small birds. But the stonechats couldn't hold them off for ever.

'Help! Help!' called out the cousins in their terrified loudest alarm calls.

Ellie took a blow on her wing and dropped down to the ground to recover for a bit. It hurt rather a lot and she felt really afraid for a moment. Then Harry swooped down. 'Are you okay, Ellie?' he chirped breathlessly, eyeballing her.

'Look out!' she trilled at the top of her voice. Harry quickly ducked a swipe from a diving magpie flying straight at him. Ellie and Harry swiftly took to the air again where they felt safer.

Sophia was dodging blows from one of the magpies and she jumped onto its back and started pecking at its neck as it flew, 'Oi! ow! ow!' it screeched in pain.

'Take that!' squawked Sophia, as she poked it with her sharp pointed beak.

Bella, seeing what Sophia had done, swooped down onto the back of a passing magpie and clutched on hard with her sharp little claws. The magpie didn't like it! 'Oi get off! Off!' it called, but Bella just held on more tightly. Secretly, she quite enjoyed the ride!

Alex and Bea had joined forces and were playing dodge the magpies together. Ege Pege, clinging onto Alex's back, was taking tiny swipes at the magpies as they flew past. 'Go away!' he screamed in his high-pitched little voice. The two cousins worked as a team, baiting the bullies and then swooping away at the last minute as the magpies tried to swipe at them. It certainly annoyed them. One of the magpies lost its balance and dived beak first into the sand. It shook its head and took off again once more in pursuit.

But all the little bird cousins were getting tired – nothing seemed to deter the magpies from attacking them.

And then, suddenly, seemingly from nowhere, Druego swooped into the middle of the fray riding an enormous black majestical bird.

'Caw! caw!' screeched the raven, wide winged, wheeling towards the magpies. Druego belted them away from the little birds with his right arm and fist. 'Go away!' he screamed in his ugly gruff voice. 'Get lost! Get out of here!' he yelled.

One of the magpies took a blow on the head from the goblin and it dropped to the ground, stunned. Druego swiped at another magpie who took a hit on his wing and swerved away from the battle and fell awkwardly to the ground, damaged. Druego battled on with great skill and strength.

And then, at last! At long last, just when things seemed to be escalating into dangerous chaos, Magic Joe riding Ray zoomed into view. Ellie glanced up and saw an enormous dazzling white bird with a huge wing span, flying straight towards the general melee. And there! There was Magic Joe with his magic wand held high, circling round his head.

'STOP!' yelled Magic Joe at the top of his voice. 'By the magical powers of the Natural World, I command you to stop! STOP!'

Chapter 27

There was silence.

The magpies, the stonechats, Druego and Rooaz landed on the ground and stood stock still. They weren't paralysed, but the magic had stopped them in their tracks, and they couldn't actually remember what they were doing before! And nor did they feel like doing it any longer.

Ray flapped his wings and landed down in the middle of them all. Magic Joe and Ege Pege dropped onto the sandy soil and stood in the centre. Magic Joe was still pointing his wand at them all. One magpie still lay stunned and everyone looked at him rather anxiously. Such a beautiful creature.

Several minutes passed while all the birds breathed slowly and calmed down. Ege Pege dismounted and looked around anxiously for his brother Ogo Pogo.

'Now then!' commanded Magic Joe 'let us all calm down. Perch down on the ground there everyone. Be still and stay quiet.'

'And now, now I want you to tell me about that necklace, you magpies.'

The birds all squatted down, rather relieved to be still for a bit. The little ones were exhausted and they gathered together near Rooaz and Druego. It seemed strange to them that now they seemed to feel safe around that goblin. But he had done so much to help them in the battle.

A magpie hopped up to Magic Joe and bowed his head.

'My name is Sorrow', he slowly cawed. 'I can tell you nothing good. Only that someone died and something was lost.'

Sorrow raised his head slowly. There was a deep sadness about him. Alex was thinking that anyone would be a sad character if they were called 'Sorrow'. *'What a dreadful name to have.. no one would ever expect you to be happy, so you wouldn't be!'*

All the little stonechats and Magic Joe looked at Druego with sympathy. They thought they knew what Sorrow the magpie was referring to.

A second magpie spoke up. 'My name is Joy. Something was found. Bright and beautiful!'

Druego looked at that magpie intently.

The third and fourth magpies spoke up together. Our names are 'Girl and Boy' – we are the children of Sorrow and Joy. We don't know very much at all.'

The fifth and sixth magpies spoke up. 'I am Silver and this is my brother Gold – we find things to put in our nests... that way we make them pretty.'

The little bird cousins then remembered the special old rhyme they had learnt about magpies:

'One for sorrow, two for joy,

Three for a girl and four for a boy,

Five for silver, six for gold...'

And then, they looked at the last magpie lying on the ground, still breathing but knocked out, and they all knew who it was.

It was the seventh magpie called 'Secrets Never to be Told.'

'Magic Joe, dear Magic Joe, can you make that magpie better so that he can tell us the secrets of Druego's missing parents?' cheeped Sophia.

'Yes! Please, Magic Joe!' chirped Bella. 'It could help Druego so much!'

And they all looked at Druego and a strange thing seemed to have happened. The goblin wasn't really looking so very ugly at all any more. His greasy yellow and green skin had become quite dry and normal looking. Best of all, that revolting, disgusting smell had vanished. A real change had come over him. All the little birds noticed it.

'I wonder if Druego's good deeds are beginning to change him,' thought Bea. *'I wonder if the fact that we are all working together to help him is making him into a nicer goblin? Or is it that we just don't notice his nastiness any longer?'*

But then Magic Joe shook his head sadly. 'Now listen children. That magpie will not tell us his secrets. He is the seventh magpie and his secrets can never be told.' Magic Joe waved his wand over the magpie and it raised its head, and then sat up with his beady eyes looking rather confused at the assembled company. It never spoke.

'We know from Sorrow,' continued Magic Joe, 'that someone died and something was lost, and I think we can all guess what he was referring to. So now comes the part that we have come here for. I want you, Silver, to tell us the story of the silver necklace with the ruby in the centre of it. And remember, we are all friends here, and not one of us, nor one of you, is going to come to any more harm. Do you understand?'

Chapter 28

'Well, Sir,' started Silver in a bright shiny cawing voice. 'You see, many years ago, the story goes that our grandparents brought the silver necklace to these woods from a far-away place. They were very proud of it. So proud of it that they made the mistake of boasting about it to any nearby birds or creatures who would listen to them. But of course, they guarded it well. It stayed up there in the trees in the nest they built. They found other treasures as well, over the years, but never anything as splendid as that necklace.'

'One day two goblins came to these woods. They told my grandparents that they were looking for their son. They were very tired and wretched. They had been searching for many weeks. But they said they had heard that the two magpies had a ruby and silver necklace, and wanted to know if it was the same one that they had given their son before he disappeared. They asked if they could see it. Well, my grandparents, being soft hearted, did show it to the goblins, who confirmed that it had once belonged to them and then their son.'

'So why is it still here, with you lot?' interrupted Ege Pege in his squeaky, grumpy voice. 'Why didn't your grandparents give it back to the goblins?'

'Well, that's the strange thing!' cawed Silver. 'The two goblins said they didn't want it. They said for us to take special care of it while they searched the world for their son. If they ever found him, they would come back for it. And, if ever he came to these woods, the magpies should give it to him as a keep-sake to remind him that his parents had always loved him. But the goblins never did come back, and I don't think they ever will. We have no idea where they are and they would be quite old by now. It is something Secret knows, but will never tell us. He can never tell his secrets. We were protecting the necklace and just wanted to stop you from taking it – we didn't know who you were. We've been guarding it from thieves and robbers all these years. The story has been passed down each generation and we have always hoped one day that its rightful owner would turn up.'

Bea looked rather sheepish. She knew she should not have taken the necklace from the Magpie's nest. She had not followed Magic Joe's instructions. He looked at her now and she felt ashamed.

Of course, only Harry and Ogo Pogo knew she had taken it. Sophia cheeped excitedly, 'Well that's wonderful! All we have to do now is find it in the nest and give the necklace back. THIS is the goblin that those parent goblins were looking for! This is Druego, the true owner of the necklace. Let's go and get it right now! Which nest is it in, Silver?'

All the magpies looked relieved. They looked at Druego and they looked at Magic Joe, they looked at all the little birds, they even looked at Ege Pege, and they looked at Rooaz and Ray and started chattering and smiling all at once (all except for Sorrow who never did such a thing). They were happy for the goblin. They had been guarding the necklace all these years and now it seemed its rightful owner had come at last.

'Wait a minute everyone!' twittered Bea at the top of her voice. 'The necklace isn't in the nest any more – Harry and I found it. I took it. I – I know I shouldn't have and I'm truly sorry. But we have hidden it in a safe place!'

'Hold your horses!' chimed in Ege Pege in his imperative bossy little voice. 'I seem to have lost my brother Ogo Pogo and I'm hopping up and down with worry about him. Where is he? Has anyone seen him? Last time I knew anything, he was with you Harry!'

Alex, Bella, Sophia and Ellie all looked mystified. 'Yes, where is Ogo?' cheeped Alex anxiously.

'Wait here!' replied Harry. 'We'll be back in a minute!'

And he and Bea flew off to the woods again and disappeared from view.

Chapter 29

The group waited anxiously. All the birds were rather tired and stood on one foot and then the other, not saying much, just the odd cheep here and there. They were getting hungry again too. There was a quietness all around.

Then, suddenly out of the woods returned the two little birds at top speed. They swooped and glided straight down into the middle of the group. There sitting on Harry's back was Ogo Pogo looking extremely pleased with himself!

'I've been terrifically brave!' he squeaked. 'I must have saved the day again!'

Everyone took a deep breath as Druego gently took the necklace from Bea's beak.

'It IS my necklace!' he exclaimed. 'It really IS mine! Thank you everyone!'

Tears welled up in his eyes, and then started dribbling down his cheeks in small streams. He was speechless. Everyone knew by looking at him that something remarkable had taken place. He put the necklace round his neck and the glittering ruby dropped onto his chest. He stroked it and held it with his hands. He looked completely different. All his awful ugliness had been transformed and while, yes, he was still a goblin, he looked like a kind, strong and brave goblin and even a good one. He looked like the sort of goblin you could really trust. One of his great sorrows had been healed at last. Just the ownership of the necklace had somehow brought something of his parents back to him.

Magic Joe, always thinking ahead, asked all the birds to settle down for some food and drink. More cake and water were produced from the endless supply in his shoulder bag. The birds pecked hungrily at delicious morsels of cheese, apples, nuts and seeds that were scattered on the beach. They drank water from a wooden bowl that magically appeared. The magpies and stonechats chattered together amiably. A couple of the magpies apologised for being so aggressive.

'That's alright,' chirped Alex. 'I think we gave as good as we got!'

Magic Joe, Ogo Pogo, Ege Pege and Druego sat quietly together on a log a little away from the others, on the river bank. All four of them hungrily ate some cake, and drank some water from empty walnut shells. They stared absently watching the tide come in. Druego was still sniffing. Magic Joe spoke at last.

'You know, Druego, you have been a very brave and quick acting goblin today. I want to thank you for all you have done to keep everyone safe. It's been a dangerous mission and I have felt you have been my very courageous right-hand man! You were valiant and fearless in the battle with the magpies. So quick in coming to help the others. You didn't hesitate or try to hide. Your parents would have been proud of you!'

More tears sprouted out of Druego's eyes.

'I've been such a wicked evil goblin for so many years,' he sobbed. 'I'm so sorry, Magic Joe.'

Ogo Pogo chipped in in his squeaky tiny voice, 'Yes, but look here, Druego, you were only a very young goblin when everything went wrong for you. You didn't know any better and you blamed the world and everything in it, for losing what you had. It's not surprising you felt angry with everything. And it's not surprising you didn't want to tell Merry and Magic Joe about the necklace. It's a hard world sometimes, and you didn't have anyone to bring you up, teach you kind ways or care for you.'

'Yes! But we are your family now! You've got us to lean on now and we'll all be your brothers and sisters!' exclaimed Ege Pege in an encouraging little voice. 'We will all make sure you're okay from now on!'

Druego looked at the two tiny pixies, no bigger than his thumbs, he eyed up the little stonechats, and suddenly saw the funny side of what Ege Pege had just said. Was this really his 'family', this strange collection of creatures? A huge smile came over him. Then he got the giggles. Then he started laughing the most hilarious, ugliest, silliest laugh that anyone had ever heard. He had never laughed before and it was a totally new experience for him. And then before they knew it Ogo Pogo and Ege Pege were creased up in peals of tiny laughter too. Magic Joe had a huge grin on his face and all the birds were chirruping and cheeping together as they watched the tears of happiness running down Druego's cheeks. Even the Magpies were laughing in their strange cawing bird voices.

Magic Joe
Ogo Pogo
Ege Pege

By Bela 7yrs.

Chapter 30

So that's nearly the end of the story. But there is just one thing to add.

Time had indeed stood still for the rest of the family who were still on the paper chase back in Parham. Two days had passed in Magic Joe's time, but only a few minutes had elapsed back at home. Magic Joe wanted to get those children home and back to safety and warmth as soon as possible and he was pondering how.

Having said their good byes to the seven magpies, who flew off, the six little stonechats said their farewells to Druego and Rooaz.

'You will come and see us won't you!' cheeped Bea. 'You know you will always be welcome.'

'You're one of us now! Part of the family!' chirped Alex.

'Oh yes, please do!' cheeped Harry.

'And Harry and I, we only live just on the other side of these woods,' chirruped Ellie, 'so we're really nearby.'

'And if Mum and Dad ever finish Magic Merry's tree house in our woods at Parham,' added Sophia enthusiastically, 'you know you'll be welcome to stay there anytime. It's completely hidden and private!'

And they promised him tea and cake – human style.

'We're ever such good cooks when we're not birds!' cheeped Bella.

Druego thanked them all for their kindness, but said he was going to carry on with his search for his parents. He said he felt stronger and happier than he had for nearly all his life. But he wanted to carry on until he had some answers. After all, two goblins travelling about must have been seen by someone.

'But this time,' he said in his croaky voice 'I shall be kind to every creature I meet on the way, and if ever I see anyone in trouble, I shall do my best to help them.' Then he added 'and if I ever find them, I'll bring them to meet you!' He grinned his funny lopsided grin with the black teeth.

Rooaz looked at Magic Joe who winked at him and smiled kindly. 'Rooaz, you have been a good brave raven. We are so grateful to you and proud of you. And now, if you wish, you may go with Druego. Carry him for as long and as far as you wish, for while you are a free bird, I see too that you have grown to like him and consider him a good master. It will be a great adventure for you!'

Druego patted Rooaz and jumped lightly onto his back. And with that Rooaz the black beautiful raven spread his vast wings and with one jump and a flap, soared off across the river Orwell towards the other side, until he and Druego were just a black dot on the horizon.

The six little cousins prepared themselves mentally for another long flight home from Nacton to Parham. To tell you the truth they weren't looking forwards to it. It would mean flying northwards again and it's nearly always colder going in that direction. Plus, they were weary from the long day's exertions.

Magic Joe surveyed them and took out his magic wand from his bag. The little birds watched intently. There was a dead hush. Alex shivered slightly in anticipation.

Magic Joe circled the wand three times over the water and said these words in a clear sweet voice;

'Queen and Kings of all the sky

We ask for your strength to help us fly

Bring us your beauty, love and power

The gift of your presence we ask of you now.'

And then all the little birds joined in with the last words in their cheeps and trills

'Now is the time renewed by sun, to count our blessings one by one.'

Three enormous white swans flew into sight from across the river. It was as if the heavens had parted and they emerged from a brilliant and wonderful sky.

They were the largest birds the small stonechats had ever encountered and it was a thrilling sight to see them gliding so gracefully towards them their necks outstretched and their beauty and grace so evident.

The three swans emerged from a brilliant and wonderful sky.

All the little bird cousins chattered and cheeped hopping up and down on the sandy shore.

The three swans alighted onto the beach with little runs, as they folded their huge brilliant white wings into their sides. Shaking their feathers, they wagged their tails in greeting.

'Welcome!' called Magic Joe. 'Thank you for coming to our aid!'

'Well, we wouldn't have missed this for the world,' snorted one of the swans, in a hoarse deep voice. 'Would we, Rose!'

'Wasn't it a wonderful way to travel, Tom!' replied the swan called Rose.

'Much more interesting than driving a car!' said the third swan. 'Magic Joe, thank you! We are SO thrilled to see you again; it's been such a long time. Well really, since we were children!'

Magic Joe grinned at them with his wonderful warm and happy smile.

Alex piped up in an excited cheep, 'Do you mean to say that you are Rose, Tom and Joe – our parents?'

'Well, yes! I'm Joe. And we have come to Magic Joe's magic command in swan form. Oh! my goodness! You must be our children, but in bird form, right?' croaked the third swan   hoarsely.

The six stonechats started twittering and giggling, so happy and amused to see their parents.

'Wait a minute, I'm confused … Are you the grown-up Rose, Tom and Joe, or the young children Rose, Tom and Joe?' chirped Bella curiously.

'Well! We're grown up, of course!' laughed the swan, Tom. 'Why on earth would you ask that?'

'Oh! Never mind!' Sophia cheeped back. 'Mummy! Rose! Swan! We've had SUCH an adventure!

'Well, I love an adventure!' replied Rose, 'I'm so glad, you'll have to tell us all about it!'

Magic Joe intervened. 'Well now, look here everyone. It's time you went home. You can tell Rose, Tom and Joe all about it on the way home, as they fly you back to Parham. Just one more thing however, when you get back to the cut, you must ALL plunge straight into the river there where you will be restored to your children and grown-up selves. You will find you are exactly back to the moment you started this adventure. You don't want to stay as birds a minute longer than that, as you will run out of time, the magic will evaporate and you will be left in no man's land. Do you understand? You must do that straight away when you get there.'

'Oh! but...' cheeped Bella, 'I don't like being a human child. I don't like my heavy wellies and I hate the cold and mud. I want to stay as a bird!'

'Me too!' chirped Ellie. She was secretly dreading the muddy walk back from the cut.

Joe the swan looked at the two little girls. 'Come on, girls, it's my birthday today and I for one want to get home to Rose's for some birthday cake and my presents!'

'Anyway, we must do as Magic Joe asks,' croaked Rose. 'Not that I particularly fancy a plunge into that cold water either!'

'Yes! Come on Ellie! It's dad's special day, and we need to get home to celebrate!' chirped Harry.

'I promise you, you won't feel a thing,' said Magic Joe. 'And when you get back to being children and adults again, you will feel better than ever, renewed with loads of energy for that last little walk back to the house! That's a promise!'

Alex looked at Magic Joe and hopped over to him.

'Thank you,' Alex cheeped. 'It's been such a great adventure and we've loved our time with you again. We hope we will see you again soon?'

'Yes, please come and see us soon, and please give our love to Magic Merry,' put in Bea.

'We love you!' chirped Sophia.

'Oi!' squeaked Ogo. 'Don't forget about us! How are we going to get home, Magic Joe?'

'Ray and I will get you home to your matchbox on the window sill, Ogo and Ege, where you can have a good long rest, don't you worry,' replied Magic Joe. 'Alex, please could you open your window when you get home, just for a little while. Children, you might just see Ray and me flying away past the window when you get home. I'll be waving!'

So, the six little birds hopped onto the backs of the beautiful white swans. They snuggled into the soft downy part under the crooks of their huge wings at the base of the long necks. It was warm and safe. Rose took Alex and Sophia, Bea and Bella hopped onto Tom's back and Joe took Harry and Ellie. The little birds loved it. The three swans opened their wings and started beating them, which made a strange hooping sound. They gracefully ran along the beach until they took off.

And if you had been there on that river beach, happening to glance upwards, you might just have seen three tiny dots disappearing into the silvery winter sky, heading north-west towards Framlingham.

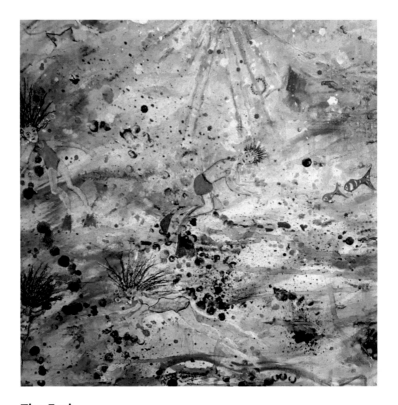

The End